BOOKS BY LESLIE FEAR

Atticus

The Graveyard Watchman

With C.D. Hussey

Villere House

Bayou Grise: Sins of Sanite

Graveyard Watchman

LESLIE FEAR

ACKNOWLEDEMENTS

FIRST AND FOREMOST, I have to thank my sweet husband, Randy. Your never-ending encouragement while managing to love me unconditionally and unselfishly has made me a better wife and a better person. You have my eternal love, even past the barn and back. <3

I must to give a huge shout out and thank you to my incredible proofreaders, Sarah Phelps and Melissa Haba. They found things even my betas didn't and I am forever grateful for their dedication and hard work!

To my beautiful friend and author, Paige Weaver. I look forward to many more lunches, brainstorming, and of course, tons more laughter. Your friendship means the world to me and I thank you for your insight on which one of my characters should become evil. ;)

To the ladies in my Graveyard Watchman Reader Group: your support, comments and constant pimping have been beyond amazing and I thank and appreciate you all so very much!

To my dear friend, Mindy Mellott, thank you for telling the world about my books! Without you, Graveyard Watchman might not have ever started trending on Wattpad in Paranormal and I appreciate everything you have and still do to support me! And remember, it's "Booooweee." <3

To my lovely mother, Sue Colburn, who will always call me "Sweetpea" and who will always be firmly planted in my heart—no matter where you are. I love you, Mom...forever.

Lastly, to my precious friend, Stephenie Thomas. Without you, I'm not sure I would have even started writing. But you wouldn't stop. You kept insisting that I give it a shot, even being painfully honest when you knew I was making excuses. I can't find the right words to explain how much I miss your laugh, your Kentucky accent or your relentless teasing, and I dedicate this book in your memory. Until we meet again, sweet girl, I hope you're dancing with the angles.

CHAPTER ONE

I'M NOT SURE how long ago it was when I first saw him, staring down at the oldest, crumbling gravestone in his black hooded cloak. He has completely captured my attention; I want to know more about the mysterious man behind all that darkness. Is he grieving like me? Maybe. It's the reason I've been coming to this God-forsaken cemetery over the last five months since Zack died.

He was my best friend and he died saving someone else's life. A firefighter's duty, I'm supposed to believe. Everyone still tries to comfort me by saying he died doing what he loved but they don't understand. I no longer have my big brother to protect me, especially from myself.

After our parents died three years ago, only blocks from our house, I became a different person. The drunk driver kept going after he plowed into them during their nightly walk. The fourteen-year-old who killed them had found his parents' whiskey stash before taking his dad's truck for a joyride. He only got two years of probation. Back then, I was upset. I was confused. I had no idea what depression was until I was in the stranglehold of its dark abyss.

My phone chirps and I look down to see a text.

Aunt Kelly: Where are you?

Shit.

Me: Be home in a few

Something catches my eye and I look up, realizing the hooded figure is now staring straight at me. There's only a slice of sun left over the horizon and he's far enough away so I can't quite make out his face, but he looks young, like me. The second our eyes lock he turns away and moves toward the forest, his heavy black cloak whipping around his body. I've never seen him move and I'm mesmerized by his powerful, athletic stride. He's got to be way over six feet tall.

I try to get a little closer but can't quite make out his features, only black hair creeping over the edges of a high collar. He glances back at me one last time, acknowledging my gasp before walking into the woods. I watch as he navigates through heavy brush until the trees and vines have swallowed him up.

Who is he? How weird is it that he's always here when I show up? I should probably be scared to death but there's something impossibly familiar about him that makes me more curious than anything. Strangely enough, I'm actually comforted by his presence and if I'm being honest, I'd be pretty unhappy if he suddenly stopped showing up.

It's pitch black outside by the time I make it back to Aunt Kelly and Uncle John's house. I live with them now since everyone in my immediate family is dead, but I try my best to stay away as much as possible. Uncle John's eyes linger way longer than any thirty-five-year-old family member's should.

The sucky part is I'm only seventeen, too young (according to the State of Texas) to be living on my own. When Zack died, my aunt and uncle took over guardianship so I have no choice. They're in charge of my life until June, which is seven long months away. At least I didn't have to change high schools.

"There you are!" Aunt Kelly pulls me into a hug before I make it fully into the kitchen. She means it; she worries about me and I know she loves me. When my mom was killed, Aunt Kelly was the only person, besides Zack, who completely understood how I felt. Mom was her sister and we were all a mess, but we had each other to lean on. I just wish she wasn't married to an asshole.

"Sorry I'm so late. I stopped by Skylar's house to get some notes," I lie. She doesn't need to know how badly my heart aches for Zack or my parents. If she did, she'd probably send me to another shrink and I know that won't work.

"It's okay, just call or text me so I don't worry, honey," she says, guiding me to a kitchen chair. "I kept your dinner warm." She places a plate full of meatloaf, mashed potatoes, and green beans in front of me. It looks good and probably is, since Aunt Kelly is a great cook, but I don't have an appetite. Not even a little bit.

"Oh, sorry, I already ate," I lie again. Her face drops, sending a surge of guilt straight to my gut, so I pick up the fork and smile. "I'm sure I can eat a few bites."

Instantly, her expression brightens as she pulls out a chair, scooting up to the table like she's ready for a chat.

I don't want to talk. I don't want to eat. I just want to go to my room and sleep. It's the only way I can escape my shitty reality.

"So, how's Skylar? Is he going out of town for Thanksgiving?" she asks, resting her chin in the palm of her hand.

"Um, I don't know, maybe. We didn't talk about it," I lie for the third time, realizing it's quiet in the house. The television isn't on and I don't see my uncle sitting on the couch with a beer in his hand.

"Where's Uncle John?" I ask, hoping I sound more genuine than I feel.

Aunt Kelly looks away, scooting back in her chair and walking over to the fridge, reaching for something inside the door. "It's poker night, remember? He's next door spending money we don't have." The resentment in her tone is loud and clear. She sets a Diet Coke on the counter and goes quiet, leaning back with a blank stare. I'm just relieved I might be saved from another two a.m. knock on my door.

Scooting the food around on my plate, I manage to make it look like I ate more than I did. Aunt Kelly hasn't moved from the counter so I take advantage, hoping she doesn't look too closely as I stand to rinse off the plate in the sink.

"You didn't eat much," she says, coming up behind me.

I look up and see the worry behind her eyes. *Shit.* I need to reassure her, and fast. I can't have her thinking I'm sinking into another black hole. She knows Zack's death cut past the underbelly of my soul and I'm pretty sure she even watches me when I'm not aware of it. She's so much like Mom it's a little creepy. I'm going to have to be more careful. My sanity depends on it. The last thing I need is her making more doctor appointments or even checking up on me with the counselor at school.

"I know, I'm sorry," I say. "Next time I'll text you if I eat before I come home." I smile, placing my fork in the dishwasher.

"You know you can talk to me," she stops just behind me as her hand lightly rubs my back, "about anything, right?"

Even her touch is like Mom's, which is strangely comforting.

"Yeah, I know. I will." I smile, hoping it's enough to reassure her. I don't want to worry her more than she already is. She has enough to deal with and I'd never forgive myself if I made things worse between her and Uncle John. Their marriage is in trouble and has been for a long time. I can see the concern behind her smile but this time when I smile back, I make sure it reaches my eyes.

"I'm going to look over the notes Skylar gave me. See you in the morning." I hug her tightly. She likes those kinds of hugs so those are the kind I always give her—especially now. I feel her head nod against my shoulder.

"Okay, sleep well."

My bedroom is just down the hallway from theirs. It's small, with only a twin bed, but it's all I need. I don't want to love this place or get too attached. As soon as I close the door and turn on the lamp, I plug in my iPhone, pushing the earbuds in place, and find my London Grammar playlist. Her voice is haunting yet graceful and it's what I need to escape my sucky world. Even for the few hours of sleep I may or may not get.

CHAPTER TWO

I'M WIDE AWAKE after only a few hours of sleep but apparently it was just enough to rev up my brain. I try like hell to will my mind to relax but it's no use. It's as if my body is attached to someone else, keeping me from the very thing I so desperately want—to avoid my shitty reality for a little while longer.

I reach around the bed for my phone and finally find it, still warm from somehow working its way under my hip. I have to turn the brightness down before I can focus and switch the music to my Mozart playlist. It's at the top, so it's easy to find. Hopefully, it'll do the trick and send me back to dreamland. It always worked when Mom played him for me as a kid. Especially when I had nightmares.

Another few minutes go by but I'm completely awake. I can't get him out of my head, no matter how hard I try. My curiosity about him is starting to make my daily trip almost a game. Will he be there today? Will he take one look at me and walk away, like he did the last time? Why is he always there? And what made him look at me when he's never even acknowledged me before? I'm not sure I'm going for Zack anymore.

I glance down at my phone and notice I have three texts messages. One from Maddy, whom I've known since sixth grade, so by default, she's also my longest friend, and two from Skylar. He's a friend, but also the guy who wants to date me even though I don't feel the same way about him. He's hot and tons of girls like him, but I just can't get past the friend stage.

My fingers automatically tap the "Messages" icon.

Skylar: Hey, thought you were coming over today. LOL

Skylar (an hour later): Did your phone die?

Maddy: Skylar's looking for you so why the fuck is he texting me?

Shit.

Even though Maddy and I had been BFF's since grade school and were practically inseparable, now she pretty much hates me. Six months ago her long-time boyfriend made a pass at me and ever since, she's been on the verge of strangling me whenever we make eye contact. Funny thing is, he made the pass at me, not the other way around. But he got to keep her and I get the bullshit he left behind.

Whatever, I don't need her, either.

I shoot Skylar a quick text, telling him I'm sorry for bailing on him but I don't give him a reason. I can't have him thinking I'm sorrier than I am but I also hate myself for being so distant. I'm not a mean person and Skylar's a good friend, but he overanalyzes damn near everything I say or do. After a while, it gets annoying and makes me want to back off from him entirely. I'm a loner. I always have been—even before my entire family died on me.

Like clockwork, my thoughts go straight back to the cemetery. He's becoming the first thing on my mind in the mornings, whether I've slept or not. It'll be hours before I can go back but this time I'm more anxious than ever to see him. He's mysterious and even a little scary but he definitely has my full attention. Maybe I should introduce myself? If he'll talk to me, that is. He's intimidating as hell, no warm or fuzzy vibes, but something makes me want to try. I can't explain it, I just want to know him.

Closing my eyes, I try to think back to the first time I saw him. It was five months ago and I was the only person left standing after his graveside service, frozen in grief, just staring at the fresh mound of dirt for hours, wiping away tears with what was left of my one dissolving tissue. I noticed his black cloak first. He stood like stone only a hundred feet away doing the same thing I was doing, only he wasn't looking at a mound of dirt, he was simply looking down, his hands crossed in the front as if praying—or maybe remembering. I'm actually surprised I even noticed him, since the rest of the service was a blur. He didn't move or even flinch as I cried for my brother.

I was already deep in a downward spiral of depression as thoughts of taking my own life were starting to flood my mind. It seemed impossible to be in this world completely alone, even being a loner and even if I still had someone left in my life who sincerely loved me.

Aunt Kelly.

But even she didn't know how dark my world had become. Ways of how I could end my misery without making a mess and not be in pain devoured my thoughts. I wanted the excruciating loneliness to end and when Aunt Kelly figured out I was in trouble, she stepped in and made my first appointment to see a shrink. That's when I knew I had to stop the horrific thoughts on my own or face months, maybe even years of therapy in some kind of psych ward until I got my shit together. Just thinking about it pricks at my gut, but it wasn't the shrink who fixed me. I'm the one who pulled myself out of that black hole and I'm the one who begged my dead brother to help me. I figured out right then that I would have to secretly suffer through the loss of my entire family on my own. I would practically have to become a different person. So on the surface, I did. I still do my best to seem healed and fine, but underneath the artificial bullshit, I hope like hell the volcano of grief swirling around in my mind doesn't suddenly erupt.

So when I finally noticed the dark man in the cemetery, it was almost a relief to shift my attention to someone I knew nothing about. Someone who made me nervous but captivated my thoughts even more than my grief.

And I'm guilty all over again...

CHAPTER THREE

I PULL MY MOM'S old Volvo in to an already packed school parking lot but manage to find a space all the way in the back. Aunt Kelly thought it was the safest of the no-longer-needed vehicles; it was also the one I was most used to driving. Every time I get in I feel closer to Mom and in a morbidly weird way, I kind of like that it still smells like her.

I reach over to grab my backpack from the passenger seat, startling when I see Skylar standing with his hands in his pockets right outside my window.

"Hey, you," he says, his expression brightening into a smile.

"Hey." I open the door, hoping he doesn't give me the third degree before school even starts.

"Walk ya to class?"

"Okay."

He falls easily in step beside me. I'm pretty sure he's about to ask why I didn't show up yesterday. I need to think of an answer and fast. He knows about my depression and takes it upon himself to constantly evaluate me.

Skylar's eyes dart over to mine and he hesitates, clearing his throat. "Everything okay?" he asks, his tone already laced with concern.

I'm not in the mood for this, I already hate the way he's looking at me, and instantly I'm pissed. I stop, which makes him do the same, and he turns to look back at me. I know he's worried that I'm slipping back into a black hole again. I know he wants to help. I can see it in his eyes and his expression confirms it.

Holy hell.

"I'm fine," I bite back, trying to calm myself down and not walk away from him. I hate that he knows that I shove every painful feeling deep inside.

"Kate," he pauses like he's trying to choose his words wisely, "you can't overcome it on your own. It doesn't work that way."

"Stop trying to analyze my every move," I practically growl, "I said I'm fine."

His face drops and I instantly feel like shit. He doesn't deserve this, he's been a good friend, but I know he wishes we were more. Ever since he tried to kiss me it's been slightly awkward between us. But I can't worry about that now. He's pretty much the only friend I have and I don't want to lose him, so I take his hand and squeeze my fingers around his.

"I'm sorry, I guess I'm just a little sensitive this morning."

He shakes his head and glances back at me. I catch the slight relief behind his eyes. "Remind me not to ask you any questions before eight," he jokes.

The mood is lifted, *thank God*, and I'm suddenly grateful he's not upset that I went off on him. Skylar's easygoing like that but sometimes I take advantage of his kindness.

I need to work on that.

He opens one side of the double doors and waits for me to step inside first. It's ear piercingly loud and the familiar smell of high school immediately hits me. A subtle combination of pencils, books, and gymnasium mixed with an overpowering aroma of perfume and cologne. It's enough to give anyone sensitive to smells a massive headache until around fourth period when it finally calms down to just plain B.O.

I make my way quickly to my locker, stuffing in my backpack as wadded up gum wrappers and loose papers tumble to the floor. I have a bad habit of using it as a trash can. Probably should work on that, too.

After the first bell rings the noise level subsides a few decibels and I notice Skylar's leaning against the locker next to me looking down at his phone. I try to be a good girl and pick up a few pieces of paper, wondering why he's still here.

"You can go," I say. "I'll see you at lunch."

He looks up at me as if he's hearing me for the first time. "Oh," he shakes his head, "yeah, okay." He smiles. "I'm playing Minecraft with a dude in Sweden. He's fucking great at it."

I roll my eyes and laugh. "Put your phone away and go learn something."

His lips curl into a smile but he doesn't look up. His fingers type something into the phone before turning it off and slipping it in his back pocket. "Okay, see ya later." He winks and walks away.

Skylar doesn't have anything to worry about, his grade point average is never below a 4.0. Hell, he's the main reason I'm passing all my classes. He's like the perfect guy—smart, good-looking, athletic—so why can't I be normal and like him as a boyfriend? I shake my head, wondering why I'm so freaking weird, and head toward my first period class. I hope my heart isn't making a huge mistake.

The last few hours of school have been torture, mostly because I've been a nervous wreck, trying to think of ways I can approach the man at the cemetery. I've even rehearsed the conversation, playing out every scenario. If he's nice, it'll be easy, but if he's not or if he's shy or combative or something, I'll probably need to back off.

Finally, the last bell rings and I can hardly wait to get to my car. Today is the day and I'm pretty sure I've gathered up enough courage to actually talk to him. I was going to tell Skylar about it at lunch but he whipped out his stupid phone and started playing his stupid game again with the stupid guy from Sweden. The plus side is, now I understand why I don't feel the way he does. Skylar's a sweetheart and I couldn't have made it through these past few years of high school without him, but in many ways, he's still just a kid. Until now, I didn't realize that I want so much more because I'm way beyond feeling like one. Not after the shit life I've been dealt.

Before I do anything, I have to drop off a book at the library. I'll still get to the cemetery earlier than normal but hopefully the extra time will help calm me down. I already have spikes in my stomach just thinking about what I'm going say.

I'm halfway to my car when I notice how much colder it is outside. The wind is picking up and I watch a flock of black birds simultaneously leap from the top of a tree as their wings create a choir of flapping sounds. Their movement is captivating and I have to pull my eyes away when my phone chirps and Skylar's name pops up.

Skylar: Chemistry notes. You still want them?

Me: Yes, can I come by later?

Skylar: I have practice after school Come at 7

Me: KK

One thing about Skylar, the boy can throw the crap out of a football. He's been the starting quarterback every year since eighth grade. The coaches were so impressed with him as a freshman they bumped him up to varsity at the beginning of our sophomore year, which doesn't happen every day, especially in Texas where football fans are borderline obsessive.

The library parking lot is bustling with people walking to and from their cars. Old people, teenagers, even a group of mothers in workout clothes pushing baby strollers. Carefully maneuvering around a man on a bike, I slow down at the return box and drop the Jane Austen book I only half read into the slot. As I pull away, I realize the sun that was shining so brightly this morning is now hidden behind a heavy bank of thick clouds. The gray hoodie I left on the floorboard a few days ago is still there and I'm grateful for my lack of organizational skills.

The closer I get the darker the skies become as little needles begin to prick at my stomach. God, I hope it's not going to rain. I'm only a couple miles away from the cemetery but I'm already starting to shake and I know it's not from the sudden chill in the air. I've got to get ahold of myself before I try to approach him. Maybe I should plan my little introduction on another day? Or maybe I shouldn't try to talk myself out of it. I've been anxious to know more about him. I have to do this. I can't back down now.

I turn onto the cemetery road, my knuckles white on the steering wheel. The same rusted iron gates greet me, creaking in the breeze. I park along the side of the road and pull down the visor to check my face. No food in my teeth and my mascara is intact.

Check.

I slowly open the car door and my hair is immediately swept up by wind, whipping it in all directions. Whatever is causing these clouds to roll in is packing a punch.

Please don't let it rain.

Pulling the hood over my head, I manage to push all my brown strands in so I can see where I'm going. Zack's grave is just over the hill and as I get closer, I see someone crouched next to a headstone, bracing themselves against the wind. My heart starts to pound in my chest. I can tell it's definitely him the closer I get. The man in the dark cloak.

So much for preparing myself.

CHAPTER FOUR

W E'RE WITHIN TWENTY feet of each other when he slowly stands, turning his face toward me. His eyes meet mine and I have to stop and catch my breath. The intense combination of brown and an almost orangey-red mix is incredible. I'm not sure if it's the cloud cover or the tiny wedge of sun somehow managing to cast light on them, but I'm mesmerized before I say a word. We stand in silence for a few more seconds while the rapid thud of my heart pounds in my ears. Then suddenly he turns and walks away.

Shit.

Did I piss him off? Does he want privacy?

I watch him head toward the woods, his heavy coat swaying in the wind, giving him an almost otherworldly look, and for a moment I wonder if he's real. Maybe he's been in my imagination all along. But then he glances back at me and I see that same rusty-red glow in his eyes, even from where I'm standing. I think he's looking back to see if I'm following him.

Wait...should I? Follow him?

I don't give myself enough time to think about it because he's about to disappear from my sight. I take off in a dead run, my feet pounding through the brush after him. My hoodie pulls away from my head, causing my thick, dark hair to scatter in all directions. I'm sure I look like a running Medusa.

The forest is dark, even without the sudden cloud cover and my eyes dart in every direction but he's no longer in sight. When I stop to catch my breath I hear the rustling of leaves and footsteps to my right. I jerk in that direction. It's him, but he's not looking at me and like before, he starts to walk away. Only this time I can tell he's actually waiting for me.

Holy shit.

I'm scared and still out of breath but I don't know what else to do. What else is there to do? So, I follow him.

Again.

Several minutes go by as I try to keep up. He's fast and knows his way around the forest, stopping only when I get too far behind.

I look up and see that the clouds have gotten thicker, making the shadows of the dense forest even darker. Lightning shoots sideways across the horizon, followed by distant rumbles of thunder. If I weren't blindly running behind some random dude in a strange forest, I'd be happy to be reading a good book in bed, snuggled under my covers. The more I think about it, the crazier it sounds, so I stop, wondering if I should go back to my car and forget this insanity.

What the hell am I doing?

Leaves crackle and the sound of a body against branches comes toward me, confirming he's on his way back. I start to panic.

What should I do? Run away? Say, "Sorry, but I don't want to play anymore?"

I barely have time to think when he's suddenly standing directly in front of me. I flinch, giving out a startled gasp. The hood of his cloak completely covers his face; all I see is dark-

17

ness when I look up. I'm frightened out of my mind but can't make myself do anything but stare. He reaches out his hand to me and there's something about his movement, something gentle and non-threatening. I hesitate because somehow I know the moment I take it, my life will change. I'm not sure if that's a good thing or not, but in an effort to relieve me of my horrible thoughts I reach out and I take it.

His hand is warm and double the size of mine and his touch sends an intense tingling vibration that shoots through my fingers and up my arm—like a small electric shock. It doesn't hurt but I'm startled and jerk my hand back as I look up. This is the closest I've been to him and I was wrong about his height. He towers over me and has to be at least six foot five. The hood of his cape still shields most of his face, but his eyes are visible and when I look a little closer, I can see specks of yellow dotted all around each auburn iris.

He reaches for my hand again and this time I'm more prepared; the tingle is still there but less severe. He pauses, as if giving me a second to get used to it, then pulls me into him, wrapping his cloak around my body. Out of nowhere, I'm lifted and carried along, safe in his arms as he easily navigates his way through the dense, narrow trail.

I'm not sure if he's running or somehow flying but whatever this is, it's fast. As quickly as he began he suddenly stops, opening his cloak to let my feet touch the ground. Everything is pitch black and I'm a little dizzy but I can tell we must be in some kind of cave because water echoes all around us and the smell of dirt and musky earth are heavy in the air. My heart races and the taste of bile hits my mouth. I'm frightened out of my mind and now I'm hoping I'm not some kind of kidnapping victim.

Trying to will the nausea away, my thoughts are quickly diverted when flames catch my eyes. Light from a primitive-looking wooden torch attached to the rock wall illuminates the area, and I see I was right. We're definitely in a cave. Rhythmic streams of rain resonate all around us, so loud it sounds almost like it's raining in here, too. But it's not.

I haven't seen him since he let go of me but I know I'm not alone. It's as if I can feel his presence. My eyes dart around, stopping when I spot a large rock with some sort of white crystals around it. He's crouched next to it, his hood down over his face.

What the hell?

I have no idea what to do next. Should I introduce myself? Should I run? There's nowhere *to* run. I can't just stand here and let him murder me without a fight.

A few seconds go by and I muster up enough courage to take several steps toward him. When I'm only a couple feet away, his palm goes up, warning me to stop.

So I do.

"Um, who are you?" I ask, hoping I haven't pissed him off already.

Silence.

Shit. This can't be happening. What the hell was I thinking? I need a plan.

Taking a few steps back, I slowly turn around, searching for the way out of here. Maybe he just wanted to keep me safe from the storm? Maybe he's just being a Good Samaritan? I'm sure I could find my way back home if I tried.

I freeze when I hear shuffling behind me. My pulse begins pounding in my ears, overpowering the sound of the rain. He's close; I can smell the earthly wool of his cloak.

"My name is Dominic."

CHAPTER FIVE

H<small>E FINALLY LIFTS</small> off his hood and looks up at me, his eyes now simply brown as tousled strands of black, shoulder-length hair stick to the side of his face in what appears to be blood. The deep gash underneath is still bleeding and my first reaction is to go to his aid. I practically leap forward, trying to cover his wound with my hand, but he grabs my wrist, holding me back.

"You must stay away." His deep voice echoes around us, pulling my eyes back to his.

"Who are you?" I ask again, my body starting to tremble.

He releases my wrist and looks away, as if trying to find the right words. "You are in danger."

"What?" I'm even more confused than before. "Who the hell are you and why did you bring me here?" I pause because the main question that's been plaguing me for months flies out of my mouth before I can stop it. "And why are you always at the cemetery when I'm there?"

He pulls himself up and I step back, wondering if I'm making him angry or worse, making him want to kill me. Clearly, he's powerful enough for the job. He carried me here like I was a feather, even though he was wounded.

We stand facing one another and I flinch when a loud crack of thunder echoes around us. The rain is definitely getting heavier, pooling in little rivers on the edges of the cave. It's little comfort, but I know I'm at least safe from the mother of a storm that's beginning to rage outside.

Finally, he slowly turns, facing the large rock with the white crystals surrounding it in a half circle. He leans down and picks one up, leaving seven remaining, and I watch it turn deep red in his fingers. He squeezes his hand and a burst of blinding white light surrounds him. It's so bright that I have to close my eyes and look away, and when I open them again, he's still standing in the same spot. I can't find words. I can't seem to do anything but watch. His head is down like he's bowing or maybe praying and I hear him whispering something I can't quite make out.

He finally turns to face me again but this time all the blood, even the deep gash, everything, is completely gone. His brown eyes have that same amber hue I saw before and now I can see his whole face. He's handsome, in a rugged, *Fight Club* kind of way and muscular, like he lifts weights. He's older than I first thought, maybe even in his mid-twenties—and there's something else, something much deeper and harder to see from just the surface. It's like an understanding, an awareness; I can almost feel the wisdom in his eyes, as if he's been in this world far longer than he actually looks.

He takes several steps toward me and stops, leaving only inches between us. He holds out both hands and I take them, looking back up at him.

"I am your Watchman." His voice is deep and soothing like his touch but I have to stay focused.

"Come again?" I don't try to disguise my disbelief as my hands begin to tremble. What is he talking about? Have I made

21

a horrible mistake? Am I now trapped in a cave with a crazy homeless dude?

His eyes narrow as if contemplating what to say next. I'm beginning to think he's just as baffled by me as I am by him. He lets go and walks away, whispering something under his breath. It sounds like it could be Latin, but he's definitely irritated.

I should probably apologize, or say something to cut the tension I'm clearly causing. So I follow behind him. He's strong, that much is clear, so maybe I should apologize before he decides to kill me.

"Look, I'm really sorry, but this is cra—"

I stop because he suddenly spins around, his black cloak catching up a second later as it flares in a circle around him.

"Listen carefully," he says, his rich voice echoing when he pauses to take a breath. "I was sent to protect you."

Holy shit. He's serious.

"I don't understand." I swallow hard, trying to push back the lump in my throat. What is he talking about? Protect me from what? Am I supposed to solve some kind of puzzle?

"You must go," he says, reaching for my hand and leading me to an archway I didn't see before. The opening is small, like a doorway, but beyond it is totally pitch back. The only reason I can see it at all is because the rocks in the wall are sparkling from the torch. I pull away. It looks scary as hell but I don't have a choice. His grip is way too strong as he pulls me through.

The same tingling sensation from when he first touched me happens again but this time, it's throughout my entire body. It's doesn't really hurt but it's not pleasant either. Kind of like when you get zapped from too much built up static electricity. Seconds later it's over and daylight is all around me. I have to squint so my eyes can adjust, but when I look up I see the same cloudy sky I saw when I walked into the cemetery. I know I heard rain in the cave (if it was really a cave and not my imagination), but everything is dry.

Wait, what?

I spin around, looking for the Watchman, or Dominic, or whoever he is, but he's gone. My hands shake but I manage to yank my cell phone from my back pocket, nearly dropping it when I tap it to check the time. I'm relieved when it quickly lights up.

Thank God it still works.

My eyes go wide when I see the time flash across the screen. 4:16. It can't be. 4:16. There's no way it's the exact same time it was when I got here. I jerk my head toward the gate and see the Volvo still parked where I left it.

What is going on?

I bolt into a dead run, heading straight for it, fumbling in my front pocket for the keys. Opening the door, I slide in, closing my eyes as I take in a deep breath, the familiar aroma of my mother surrounding me.

Calm down, calm down, calm down...

Flashes of lightning streak across the dark sky while booms of distant thunder follow closely behind. I wait for a moment, trying to piece together what the hell just happened. Did I somehow bang my head and dream everything up? My hands go to the sides of my face then the back but nothing hurts and my hands are free of blood.

This is completely nuts, or more likely, maybe I've finally lost it?

I stick the key into the ignition, looking up when something dark catches my eye.

It's him.

The Watchman.

He's standing where he always stands but this time he's facing me, like he wants me to see him. He's completely motionless—a statue—and then he vanishes into thin air.

Oh.

My.

God.

If I hadn't seen it with my own eyes, I wouldn't have believed it. Am I hallucinating? Has losing my entire family finally pushed me over the edge? Can taking Prozac for over two months cause some kind of delusional side effect?

I have no clue because my eyes are still glued to the spot, wondering if he'll somehow reappear. Is he an eccentric magician who enjoys playing sick jokes on people at cemeteries?

No, even I know that's not true, and my thoughts instantly go back to the six words he said to me.

"I was sent to protect you."

What the hell is that supposed to mean? Protect me from what? Myself? I'm not sure anyone can do that even if they *are* capable of disappearing. It feels like I'm in a never-ending black hole, trying to claw my way out and getting nowhere when I try. The psychiatrist told me it will eventually pass. He said that since I never suffered from depression before now, it'll just take time. Apparently, the kind I have is the kind people get when they die of a broken heart. Maybe he's right. I've never experienced anything this horrific before.

I hear a chirp from my phone and see Skylar's text flash across the screen.

Skylar: Come over if u want. Practice was cancelled.

A friend sounds really good right now...and he's pretty much the only one I've got. I don't even have to think about it.

Me: On my way.

I shift into reverse and back up, turning the Volvo around. I take one last look at the hill but he's not there—only flashes of lightning streak across the ominous sky.

I push the stick into drive and punch the gas, passing through the tall cemetery gates as fat raindrops begin smashing against the windshield.

A few minutes later I'm standing on Skylar's front porch, relieved to have somewhere to go after the insanity of what just happened.

He gets to the door quickly and as usual, he takes one look at me and his smile instantly drops. "What's wrong?"

How the hell does he do that?

"Nothing. Why?" I smile, trying to make it reach my eyes as I stand there, holding a broken umbrella above my head.

There's no freaking way he can ever know about the Watchman or whatever just happened. He'll go straight to talking about my depression and asking if I'm taking my medicine like he always does. I know he cares but he's like my freaking mother. I just want to talk without him analyzing my every move, but that's not going to happen. He's already taken it upon himself to watch me like a hawk.

I'm pissed before I even walk into his living room. Maybe I shouldn't have come here.

His eyes narrow like he doesn't believe me. "Fine, don't tell me. But I'll eventually get it out of you."

Good luck.

Before we can get into it, I get a text from Aunt Kelly telling me to come home before the storm hits. It's already raining and ominous-looking, so it's the perfect excuse for a super quick visit. Besides, I know he would have tried to get me to talk. I made him a promise a while ago that I wouldn't keep

25

any more secrets from him. Now I don't have to make up an excuse or worse, lie.

After handing me the chemistry notes, Skylar pulls the curtains to one side and looks out the window. "Shit, she's right, you better go."

"I know," I answer, pushing up the half crumpled umbrella.

"Seriously?" he mocks, frowning at the pathetic excuse I'm about to hold over my head to stay dry.

"Dude, don't judge me, it's only sprinkling and it's better than nothing."

"Just barely. Go—before it starts to pour."

His words haunt my thoughts. This is the same storm I already lived through once. In the cave, when I was with Dominic. The Watchman.

Shades of green and gray and even yellow blanket the sky as scary, thick clouds race above me. Now I'm on a mission to get home before all hell breaks loose. Within minutes, my cell phone buzzes.

Jesus, what now?

"Hey," I answer.

"Where are you?" Aunt Kelly asks, the urgency in her voice grabbing my attention.

"On my way home. Why?"

"There's a tornado in the area, honey. If you're closer to Skylar's, go back until it's over."

Shit.

"I'm almost home," I lie. I'm closer to his house but I can't go back. I can't be interrogated right now. Not when I can barely wrap my head around anything.

"Okay, just hurry, honey."

I hang up, trying to ignore the sky that has become almost black with fury. The rain is coming down so hard I have to slam on my breaks at a stoplight because I barely saw it. The wind rocks the Volvo and I pan around, looking for other cars, but clearly no one's stupid enough to be driving right now. I decide to run the light, hoping I can keep going without breaking the law again, at the next stoplight. But that doesn't last either. I don't even give myself enough time to think because this time I blow right through the intersection, trying like hell to stay aware, darting my eyes in every direction.

Almost there.

Relief hits me two miles later when I get to our street. It's short-lived, of course. Within seconds it sounds like a hundred pellet guns are shooting at the roof of my car as hail begins to mix in. It's deafening and I can barely make out anything even with the wipers on their fastest setting. I have to slow down because the faster I go, the less I can see.

This is crazy.

Finally, I see the driveway and turn in. Aunt Kelly is at the door, frantically waving me to come in. I don't even try to use my joke of an umbrella and practically fly up to the door, my purse and a binder over my head.

Something catches the corner of my eye as she pulls me into the house. Something in all black and maybe hooded? It happened so fast that whatever it was is gone before I can tell for sure.

Wait.

It was him. Dominic. The Watchman.

He knows where I live?

CHAPTER SIX

I DON'T HAVE TIME to think more about it because Aunt Kelly is hugging the life out of me.

"Thank God you're okay!" she says in my ear.

"I'm fine," I reply, wondering how long she'll keep me in a vice grip.

She pulls back, keeping her hands firmly planted on my shoulders. "I made soup. You hungry?"

"Yeah, sounds good," I say automatically, so deep in thought I probably would have agreed to anything.

Was it really him? Or was it just my imagination?

"Hey, cutie," my uncle says, winking as I walk past him to the kitchen.

Gross.

"Hey, Uncle John," I say with little enthusiasm. I can't stand him. He's made Aunt Kelly's life a living hell for years. Mostly because he barely works, only taking jobs here and there when he feels like it, then spending every penny of it gambling or buying beer. The other day I smelled pot when I took out the trash and I knew it was him puffing away behind the fence. He's such a loser. It's hard to see what my aunt saw in him. According to her, he was very different in high school. Back then he had goals and wanted to be a veterinarian, even went to school for a couple of years before dropping out.

Apparently, after they lost their one and only child at birth, ten years ago, everything went downhill. He wanted a son so badly and that's what he got, but in addition to losing the baby, it nearly cost Aunt Kelly her life. I think he even blames her for the baby's death. *Asshole.* Now he just survives, spending money Aunt Kelly makes working for the assistant principal at the middle school. Which isn't much.

I've thought about getting a job to help but Aunt Kelly won't allow it. She says the money Mom and Dad, and now Zack, left me is more than enough for my support. I've tried several times to give her some of my "inheritance," but she won't take any of it. Deep down I know she feels responsible for her choices, but it baffles me why she doesn't just divorce him. She's beautiful and kind and smart as hell. She could seriously have any guy she wanted. My guess is that there's too much history between them and she now feels responsible for him.

Out of nowhere, a flash of white light, instantly followed by an ear piercing crack of thunder, makes both of us jump.

"Holy shit!" Aunt Kelly shouts, her hand going to her mouth.

"I think it hit the house!" Uncle John screams, running up the stairs two at a time. "Kelly, call 911!"

She races for her phone on the coffee table and begins frantically dialing but she's pushing too many buttons. "Fucking passcode, c'mon!" Relief washes over her face when she finally punches in the correct numbers but she's breathing like she just sprinted a mile. "Hello? I—I think lightening just hit our house!" she screams, then her face contorts with fury.

LESLIE FEAR

"I'm not going to calm down while you ask me stupid questions! My house could be on fire!!" She pauses, taking a deep breath. "5311 Early Court Drive. Hurry!"

We both look up as black smoke begins to rush down the stairs in heavy, billowing waves.

"John!" Aunt Kelly screams, dropping the phone. She races to the stairs as another rush of thick smoke drifts down, stopping her from going further. "John!" her voice cracks. "John, can you hear me?"

Silence.

I run to her side to help but her hand goes up to stop me.

"No! I have to find him! Wait here." The determination in her eyes is palpable.

"Aunt Kelly, no!" I pull her arm back. "You won't make it past the first few steps!" I shout as distant sirens echo outside.

"I—I have to try, Katie!" She coughs and yanks her arm from my grip but I manage to grab her other one as she turns.

"No!" I cough. "You can't, it's too—"

I'm interrupted when three firefighters burst through the front door.

Thank God.

"You need to evacuate immediately!" one of them shouts as flashing red and white lights circle outside, reflecting off the heavy smoke filling up the living room.

Aunt Kelly drops to her knees, her hands over her face. "My husband! He's upstairs but he's not answering me!"

One of the firefighters scoops her up. "We'll find him, ma'am, but you have to get out, now!" He turns, holding her like she weighs nothing, and sprints toward the door. The other wraps me up in his arms, practically flying me outside, then sets me down next to Aunt Kelly on the curb.

His eyes are familiar. "Stay here!" he says firmly.

Wait...

Holy.

Shit.

The same brownish-red stare. I'm sure he wanted me to see him. I continue staring as he rushes away, disappearing in the house.

I start to tremble. I'm not sure if it's shock from the fire that has Uncle John trapped or the fact that I was just recused by him.

The Watchman.

Aunt Kelly sobs in my arms. The roof is almost completely gone and I start to wonder if Uncle John is already dead. I don't like him but I don't want him to die. It would destroy Aunt Kelly to go through another loss, no matter how bad their marriage is.

Everywhere I look is complete chaos. Neighbors are gathered in their front yards, trying to get a better view. Firefighters are darting in and out of the house while others aim huge water hoses at the roof. But strangely enough, it all seems to be going in slow motion, even as a neighbor from across the street rushes over with a blanket, draping it over us.

Finally, one of the firefighters shoots out of the front door, carrying Uncle John's lifeless body.

Aunt Kelly takes off. "Oh my God, John!" she screams, running to his side.

Another firefighter gets to her before I do, holding her back from her husband, and we watch in disbelief while two of them perform CPR.

"I'm not getting a pulse!" one of them shouts. The paddles used to shock someone's heart are slammed to his chest.

"Clear!" the other says as Uncle John's body tenses up and goes lifeless again.

"Nothing! One more time!" the one holding the paddles calls out. "1...2...3. Clear!"

This time, one of them looks up and says, "We have a pulse! Get him in the ambulance now!"

"I'm going with you!" Aunt Kelly insists, then turns to me with tears in her eyes. "Katie, I'm sorry, I have to go. I have to be with him."

"Go! I'm okay!" I reply, giving her a quick hug. "I'll be fine."

She pulls away, shooting me a half smile before climbing into the ambulance. I watch her take Uncle John's hand as she leans down to kiss his forehead. He doesn't move. The double doors slam shut and the sirens begin to blare as the ambulance speeds away.

I'm still wondering if all of this actually just happened when I get a tap on my shoulder.

"Let's get you checked out." A firefighter guides me to the remaining ambulance as two men effortlessly hoist me up, placing me on an ice-cold gurney.

"I'm fine, really," I protest, looking into the green eyes of a man who's not the Watchman. Where is he? Did he vanish like before?

"We're going to check your breathing," the firefighter insists. "Protocol. Just relax."

Strangely enough, I'm no longer trembling and feel numb all over as something gets wrapped around my left arm. One of them is asking questions but his features are starting to blur and I can't speak. I can hear his words, but it's like my body is on lockdown and I'm trapped, waiting for it to release me.

"She's in shock," he says, looking up to the other guy.

"Hurry, let's get her on an I.V.," the first guy says as he gently lays me down on the gurney.

"Elevate her legs," the other one orders, handing him a pillow.

"Kate, can you hear me?" the first guy asks but I can't answer him. "Hang on." He looks around as if realizing something then looks up at the house. "Is her last name "Bassett?"

"Holy shit," the other one whispers, placing a blanket over me. "She's Zack's sister."

"Dear God." The first guy shakes his head. "Can anything *else* go wrong for this family?"

"Let's get her to the hospital. She may need a breathing treatment, too."

"Agreed," he replies then looks down at me. "Kate, we're going to take good care of you. Just hang on."

A few blurry hours later I'm released from the hospital and advised to get some rest. The guys in the ambulance must have said something to the hospital staff because no one made me sign papers or pay for anything. I'm not sure if my brother's death had anything to do with it but I'm grateful for the charity all the same.

I still feel shaky and just want to go to bed but I can't. What bed would I go to anyway? I need to find Aunt Kelly. I actually hope Uncle John is okay because it feels like my life, hell, my reality is spinning out of control.

The storm.

The lightning.

The fire.

The cemetery.

The Watchman...

I mean, what the hell is going on? Am I cursed?

I walk up to the lady behind the receptionist's desk. She's busy typing something on a computer and doesn't even look up.

"Excuse me. Can you tell me the room number for John Jacoby?"

She looks up at me like I've just asked the most ridiculous thing she's ever heard. "Sorry, I don't have that information. This is the Emergency Room." Her sarcasm practically floats in the air.

"Oh, um, okay, where can I get—"

"Connie," the nurse who treated me appears to my right, "give her his room number!" she demands. "For Christ's sake, her house was on fire!"

The look on Connie's face is pure resentment but I don't care, I need to find Aunt Kelly. She looks back to me and tilts her head. "Room 402," she points to my right, "is just down the hall."

I don't hesitate or even thank her as I quickly make my way toward his room. As soon as I get close, I stop just outside the door and listen. One of the doctors is telling Aunt Kelly that Uncle John will have to stay a couple more days for observation. Apparently, he's being treated for severe smoke inhalation and second degree burns on his right arm and leg. Relief washes over Aunt Kelly's face when the doctor finally tells her that Uncle John will be okay. It's almost as if his words have suddenly given her permission to pull away from her bedside vigil. I know her well, and it's obvious she feels somehow guilty. Maybe even believing that she should have been the one who ran upstairs to check on the house—and now she's punishing herself for it. I hate seeing her this way. I hate that she always tries to take all the blame.

She doesn't notice me until the doctor leaves the room, but when she does, her face instantly lights up. Then she leans down and whispers, "I'll be back soon, honey," and kisses sleeping Uncle John's cheek.

The second she turns back to me, I rush into her arms, tears coursing down my cheeks. Her hand cups the back of my head and I can barely hear her words. "Thank God you're here," she says into my hair. "Thank God. I don't know what I would have done if anything had happened to y—"

"I'm okay," I say, interrupting her. "I'm okay."

She starts to cry and hugs me a little tighter. "I—I'm not sure what to do." She sniffs. "I mean, I think we still have a few things we can salvage, but from what they told me..." She pauses and hiccups. "The house is a total loss."

"It'll be okay," I assure her. "We'll figure it out. Now, will you please let me help you?"

Aunt Kelly pulls back and looks me in the eyes. "What do you mean, honey?"

"We need a place to stay, don't we?" I say, smiling through the tears streaming down my cheeks.

Her face contorts into a half happy, half concerned expression as she pulls me into her usual tight hug again. "Yes. Yes, we do, sweet girl."

CHAPTER SEVEN

"HERE YOU GO," the older lady behind the motel front desk says, holding out two key cards.

I take them and smile. I'm happy to finally have a decent bed to sleep in after two nights on a hard sofa in Uncle John's hospital room.

"You're paid up for the rest of the month. If you need your rooms for longer, just let us know."

I nod and walk back out to my car. Aunt Kelly is waiting in her Explorer with Uncle John, who looks asleep and is most likely high on pain meds. She's wiping her eyes.

"Are you okay?" I ask, hoping the concern on my face doesn't reveal how frightened I really am. She doesn't need that extra burden right now.

"Oh, yeah, honey." She quickly hides the Kleenex I already saw. "I just hate that you're having to use your inheritance money." She looks over at Uncle John, then back to me, and whispers, "He doesn't know this, but I managed to put a little money away for emergencies… It's not—"

I interrupt her guilt trip. "Aunt Kelly, this was my choice and I want to help. Besides, you really don't have a choice—my mind's made up." I smile a little wider and watch the hesitation on her face subside. "Here," I hand her their suite card key, "I was able to get a room right next to yours."

After getting Uncle John settled in bed, Aunt Kelly manages to make a quick grocery run before stopping by the house to pick up the salvaged clothes a few of the neighbors gathered from our closets. It was really nice of them and I'm happy to have a few sets of newly washed clothes.

The tiny kitchenette doesn't have an oven but there's a hot plate for stovetop cooking, a microwave, small fridge, and a coffee pot. All the basic essentials needed until we figure out what to do from here. I can afford a lot more but Aunt Kelly insisted on something simple and functional. I know cooking dinner is her attempt at keeping things as normal as possible, and I'm grateful for her all over again.

"I'm gonna grab a shower and go to bed," I say as I take the last bite of my chicken. "Let me help you clean up."

"Nope. I got it, honey, get some rest," Aunt Kelly says, kissing my cheek as she gives me a quick hug.

"Okay, text me if you need me," I whisper, glancing over at Uncle John, still passed out from pain meds, before letting go.

♣

My room isn't fancy but it's clean and there's a thick white robe hanging on the back of the bathroom door. It's too big but that makes it more comforting as I wrap it tightly around my body and slip into bed.

I'm exhausted but the second I close my eyes, horrific images of the past 24 hours slam into my head. I wonder if this is what Post Traumatic Stress Syndrome feels like. Reaching for the remote, I flip through channels, eventually finding an old movie—anything that might help take my mind off today.

But it's no use.

I can't stop thinking about the firefighter. He was the Watchman or wait, Dominic—I need to figure out what the hell to call him. The fact that he miraculously showed up and carried me out of our burning house makes me question everything. How did he know I was in trouble? How was he there at just the right time? I need to find him. I need answers. I have to go back to the graveyard as soon as possible. I know he'll be there.

I can almost *feel* him.

♣

I wake up to a sound I'm not used to and have to think for a second before realizing where I am. A moderately expensive motel where people stay for business trips or family reunions, not because their house burned to the ground—along with everything else they own.

I fumble around for my cell phone, thankful the neighbors found my charger, and plug it in on the table next to me—the one with the touch-on lamp and a Bible tucked inside the drawer. I push the toggle button, but have to squint when the bright screen flashes on. It's nearly two in the morning and I've only been asleep for maybe an hour. No huge surprise. This isn't my bed and these aren't my sheets.

It's starting to feel like my life is spinning out of control. *Again.*

Only now I've lost even more. It's like the fire was the universe's final blow in its quest to drive me bat-shit crazy, well on my way back to being borderline suicidal. I can't take much more.

After Zack died and the gravity of losing another family member, not to mention my best friend, actually sunk in, I felt the anxiety and depression creeping up my spine like a snake waiting for the right moment to strike. The same slithering snake, hiding just beneath my already unstable thoughts, seems to be growing. Those thoughts never left, they just became diluted by new chaos, the kind of chaos that not only confuses me but also scares the shit out of me.

The Watchman.

Who is he? Why is he watching me? And hell, is he even human?

All I know is he keeps showing up when I least expect it, like freaking Superman but way bigger and much darker. I'm not sure if it's evil I feel or just his sheer power. He spoke to me. Told me his name. But I need to know more. There's only one way to find out and I'm pretty sure I know where to go. I'll never sleep until I get some answers.

I toss off the covers and touch the base of the lamp. The light is blinding for a second but I manage to find my car keys and slip on my jeans and red sweater without crashing into anything. My heart is practically pounding out of my chest, the thud deafening in my ears. It's so loud I'm grateful only I can hear it as I carefully open the door, completely unaware that my life is about to change forever.

CHAPTER EIGHT

I START THE VOLVO, checking my phone while I wait for the seat to warm up.

Skylar: Holy shit! Just heard what happened! R U Ok?

Skylar: Kate, where are U?

Skylar: Call me!

I look at the time stamps and realize he's been sending them since yesterday morning.

Shit.

Me: Dude, I'm an orphan AND homeless 2.

I meant to be funny but I'm not sure he'll take it that way so I type "LOL" and hit send.

Ten seconds later my phone chirps, startling me out of my thoughts.

Skylar: Where are U? And why RU up so late?

Me: Holiday Inn Suites on N. Main. Can't sleep.

Skylar: Will you be at school today?

Crap. School hasn't crossed my mind since Friday when I took my physics test. It's the last place I want to be right now.

Me: No, I'm gonna need a couple days. Thx for the reminder. I'll tell Aunt Kelly to excuse me.

Skylar: It's only a half day before Thxgiving break. U won't be missing much.

Thank God.

Skylar: Need anything? I'm available if you want a shoulder to cry on.

He's serious, too, but I know if I take him up on his offer it'll send the wrong message. I adore Skylar, but I don't want to be his girlfriend. I never have. As nice of an offer as it is, it wouldn't help our "situation" any.

Me: I'm okay, THKS, gonna try to sleep. Text ya later.

Skylar: KK. Text me any time day or night.

Whew...another potential problem diverted. I don't need to be the center of attention at school. I can't handle people staring at me with their faces full of pity. Not again.

Check.

I put the Volvo in reverse and pull out of the parking lot, heading straight for the cemetery. The nighttime sky seems darker than usual but it's weirdly comforting, like it's somehow shrouding me. Could all of this just be a bad dream?

God, what I wouldn't give...

I tremble as sharp pins begin poking around in my stomach. I probably shouldn't be doing this—driving to my brother's grave to get answers from a strange man, or whatever he is. I'm not even sure I'll get them. My fingers grip the steering wheel so tightly they start to ache and the further I drive the more nauseated I get. Should I turn around? Should I forget I ever saw him? He saved my life...don't I owe him a thank you? No, that's not even close to the truth. I want to see him and it's not the answers I crave.

It's him...

Who is he?

Where did he come from?

41

Why me?

I slowly pull through the cemetery gates. I can only see a few headstones just in front, reflecting off my headlights. It's too damn dark to see anything beyond them, so I put the car in park and reach for the flashlight in the glove box. My mother always kept one for emergencies. Not sure this is an emergency but I do know I'll go completely insane if I don't find out what's going on—and soon. I test it and it works...*thank God.*

The air here is completely different than it was at the hotel. There it was somewhat breezy and dry but now it's the polar opposite. There's zero wind and it's chilly and wet, like rain might be coming.

That's strange.

Shrugging it off, I try to focus on the task at hand. Finding the Watchman.

Gravel under my feet disrupts the quiet night, or, morning, actually. Wait a minute. I don't hear crickets or birds or anything. That's weird. This place is as silent as a padded room.

My heart starts to beat faster and I'm not sure if it's because I'm visiting my brother's grave in the dead of night or I'm just starting to freak out. It doesn't take long for the goosebumps to ripple up my arms. I stop in my tracks when my flashlight finds him crouched down in front of Zack's headstone.

Calm down, Kate. Calm down.

I stand frozen, keeping the light on his back, but he's completely wordless as I stare. Seconds that feel like minutes go by before he finally stands up. I can't see his face but I'm astonished all over again at his enormous size.

"Turn it off," he says, his voice low and deep.

Without a word, I look down and immediately hit the off switch and toss the flashlight to the ground. When I look up, he's facing me, but all I see is the outline of him. He then slowly turns to walk away, looking back as if checking to see if I'm following him.

And I am...

CHAPTER NINE

THE AIR REMAINS damp and there's still no sound of crickets or even birds, but after my eyes adjust I can just barely see. I don't have time to think any further because the Watchman is darting in and out of trees and brush so quickly I have to stay aware of his every move. And like before, we're definitely following a well-established, albeit hidden, path. Occasionally, he looks back to make sure I'm keeping up.

I swear we've jogged a mile and we're still going. My side is beginning to cramp and I need to take a break so I slow down and stop, leaning against a tree as I try to catch my breath. Out of nowhere, I'm scooped up under a black cloak or a wing or something. I can't be sure because as quickly as I'm up we stop and I'm down on my own two feet again.

What the...

I hear shuffling and what sounds like flapping, as if a giant bird is nearby. My attention is drawn to a flicker of light on a torch anchored to a stone wall. Then another. My eyes quickly scan the area and I realize we're back at the cave. The Watchman stands before me. As usual, I only see his black shape and of course, he's silent. I'm scared but not in a frantic way, even though he makes me nervous as hell. For whatever reason, this feels safe.

"W-who are you?" I get out.

"I told you who I am." His familiar deep voice resonates throughout the cave.

"The Watchman? Yeah, um, you're gonna need to give me more than that."

"I was sent to protect you," he says, not moving.

"Okaaay. But, why? And by who?" I ask, trying not to offend him with too many questions.

"Zack," he responds, walking toward the large rock with the lines of crystals surrounding one side.

It feels like my heart drops into my stomach I'm instantly nauseated. Then it picks back up, beating so fast and so loud I'm sure he can hear it. "Wait, what? My brother? That's impossible. He's dead."

"No," the Watchman replies, "he is one of us."

"You aren't making sense!" I shout as I stomp toward him, every emotion I haven't let go of for months slamming to the surface. "Stop screwing with me! My brother was my life and he's buried in that grave I visit almost every single day!" My screams echo loudly along the walls.

His head shifts and he looks over at me, locking his eyes with mine. I see their slight yellow glow underneath his black hood.

"He has come for you..."

"What do you mean, he's come for me?" I spit out. "Who's come for me?"

The Watchman turns around, kneeling to pick something up, then takes three long strides in my direction. He reaches out, and without thinking, I open my hand, allowing him to drop a cool metal chain. I know exactly what it is and my face

45

gets hot as my heart begins to pound with fury. It's the gold necklace Aunt Kelly gave Zack to commemorate his graduation from the fire academy. He wore it every day and I know without a shadow of a doubt he was wearing it the day we buried him. I squeeze the necklace in my hand, slammed with a flood of emotions as my entire body starts to shake.

"Where did you get this?" I ask as tears stream down my cheeks.

"You must trust me," he says quietly.

"Trust you? Are you insane? You stole my brother's necklace off his dead body and you want me to trust you?" I shout, the heavy echo of my shaky voice catching up a second later.

The Watchman's eyes go from a brownish yellow to a deep red when he jerks his body several steps away from me, almost like he had to stop himself from hurting me. I flinch and back up against the rocky cave wall, my fingernails digging into the flesh of my palm as I grasp Zack's necklace with all I have. I don't care what he does to me, there's no way he's ever going to take it away from our family again.

"Katie." A familiar voice comes out of nowhere.

My breath hitches and I barely notice the cry that escapes. I know that voice. I know who called my name. My eyes frantically scan the cave. I heard him. Where is he?

"Zack?" I get out as a flash of brilliant light illuminates the dim cave, making me cover my eyes. I lower my arm cautiously, squinting at the figure of a man standing only feet away, dressed in the same kind of cloak as the Watchman.

"Yes," he answers and before I know what I'm doing, I'm running, jumping straight into his arms as mine go snugly around his neck.

"Oh my God, Zack!" I whisper between sobs. His arms pull me closer and the tears overtake me. I can hardly catch my breath. A distant fluttering of wings clips my attention but I don't care. My brother is alive and that's all that matters right now.

CHAPTER TEN

ZACK FINALLY LETS go and I reluctantly pull back to study him, still in shock that he's standing right in front of me. Something is off. The shape of his face is different, or maybe it's his hair. I squint, hoping it will help me focus a little better, but it's difficult—the light in here is dim as hell. I see it when we lock eyes. His are no longer a deep brown, but a luminescent cobalt blue. It's as if they're somehow backlit.

Holy shit.

Had I not heard his voice before I saw his face, I'm not sure I would have recognized him right away.

"What happened to your eyes?" I blurt out.

Zack looks over to the Watchman then back to me. "Everything will be explained to you but for now, you must listen to me," he answers, confusing me even more.

"Wait, what the hell is going on, Zack? I saw your body in the coffin! How are you alive?"

"Katie," he says in a calming whisper and instantly my stupid tears are back. He's the only person in the world who calls me that.

"I have sent Dominic to protect you," he explains.

I glance over at the Watchman, who remains expressionless, then jerk my eyes back to Zack, his crazy-beautiful stare distracting my thoughts for a second before I remember what I wanted to say.

"I don't need protection," I insist. "I'm fine. I—"

"Actually, you do, trust me." He pauses and takes my hand. It's cool to the touch, making me question if he's even real.

"Why is everyone saying I need to trust them? Trust you for what? Is there gonna be some kind of zombie apocalypse or something?" I don't try to disguise my frustration or sarcasm.

"I have to go," he says, patting my shoulder. He looks past me and nods. "Dominic, take her back."

"Wait, no!" I shout. "You can't leave! I just got you back!"

The Watchman does what he's told. Without hesitation, he drapes his cloaked arms around me, cocooning me against him. This time I can actually feel wings fluttering as they shape around my body. What is he—some kind of giant demonic bird? I try to wiggle and call out to my brother but it's too late. I can't move or speak. There's no sound, not even wind, and I'm completely surrounded by blackness. It feels like I'm floating or maybe flying. As soon as I try to scream, I'm jarred to my feet as a cool breeze hits my face and my eyes flash open. We're outside, because I can smell the musty, damp earth but a cloud of disorientation blankets my vision like a thin veil. I shake my head, hoping to clear the remaining fog. I'm pretty sure we landed next to Zack's grave but it's difficult to keep my balance. Everything is wobbly as the landscape winds down, spinning at a sickening speed. I stumble forward, rocking against a hard chest. Strong hands catch me under my arms. I turn around and look up, trying to focus on the Watchman holding me.

"Easy..." he says in his low, rich voice, steadying me as I desperately attempt to keep myself from throwing up.

Somehow his words steady the rotation, or maybe I'm distracted, but for the first time there's enough moonlight (or maybe I'm close enough) to make out his entire face. His strong, rugged features captivate me, sending a quick pulse between my legs as his caramel-colored eyes gaze down at me with obvious concern.

"It will pass," he says.

"Um, how...?" I get out, but he's already let go, scanning the area like he's making sure we're alone. To my surprise, I'm not entirely sure I want him to release me, so I grab his hand. His face jerks back to me. We lock eyes and I can see the alarm in his gaze.

"Do you need more time?" he asks, cocking his head at my unexpected move.

"Yes...I mean, maybe. I'm not sure," I admit, still gripping his massive hand. My next question is out before I know I've asked. "Where's Zack?"

The Watchman looks at his feet, as if trying to find the right words. "He is not your concern right now," he answers in a controlled, almost matter of fact, tone.

"What? Not my concern? He's my brother. Where is he?" I pause, waiting for him to answer, but he doesn't. He lets go of my hand and backs away, like he's afraid to be so close to me.

"We don't have much time. You need to go," he says, darting his eyes around again and suddenly, I'm pissed. Really pissed.

My hands automatically go to my hips but he doesn't notice—he's still being weird, watching every wind-blown leaf as if it's about to attack us.

"I'm not moving until I get some answers. This cryptic shit needs to stop!" I shout, realizing that raising my voice was a really bad idea. It's the middle of the night and we're in a public place. I watch his face change and what I see next makes the hair on my neck stand up. His eyes go from caramel to bright red as something from behind him, maybe on his back, lifts his body. He quickly crouches over me like he's shielding me and my world goes completely black.

CHAPTER ELEVEN

THIS TIME I'M fully conscious, flat on my stomach under his cloak, but I can't see even a speck of light. I flinch when violent, animalistic growls take over the silent night air. The Watchman's body huddles closer to me as more guttural snarls come from every possible direction. I'm too frightened to move, the pounding of my heart a deafening boom in my head.

Out of nowhere, the sounds of shooting flames and large flapping wings crash through the air. I question my own sanity as my eyes dart from side to side, trying to follow the shrieks above us, mentally picturing mythical creatures I've only read about in books.

What the hell?

"You cannot have her!" a familiar voice shouts.

Wait, was that Zack?

I want to call out for him but know I shouldn't. I'm trapped and pretty sure he and the Watchman are protecting me from someone or more likely some *thing*.

Seconds go by like hours; I can only imagine the terror going on above me. The Watchman's body is practically lying against mine, maybe only a thread separating us. His body was warm and comforting at first but now I'm beginning to sweat with heat and panic. Claustrophobia doesn't even cover it. I sigh with relief when a slight pop of cool air hits my face.

Without warning, the black shield keeping me in the darkness disappears, the cold night air as still as before. I frantically look around as I lift myself into a sitting position, finally spotting two figures just behind me. One is Zack and the other is the Watchman, using Zack as a crutch. He's bent over and it seems that his breathing is labored, like he can't catch enough oxygen.

"Zack!" I shout and they both snap their heads toward me as I jump to my feet.

"Katie!" Zack raises his hand. "Stay back!"

I freeze in place as his attention goes back to the Watchman.

"You must take another crystal," Zack says to him.

And then I see it. The Watchman's cloak is ripped to shreds, completely covered in blood, a mist of steam billowing from several deep gashes on his back. The Watchman nods, glancing over at me, his eyes glowing that bizarre reddish hue as they shift back to Zack.

"I'll take care of her, now go!" Zack waves his hands like wands and incredibly, the Watchman is gone. Only the stench of burning flesh remains. If I hadn't seen it with my own eyes I wouldn't have believed it.

Zack turns toward me, taking cautious steps in my direction. "It's okay, Katie. It's over...for now."

"What do you mean it's over for now?" I demand, staring at my brother, who still looks like a completely different person. "What's over? What the hell was that?"

He pauses after a few steps, rubbing his chin like he's trying to find the right words, then turns back to me. "We need to talk, Katie."

"Ya think?" I say, knowing my sarcasm accentuates how frustrated I am.

"We can't do it here. We..." He pauses, scanning the area, his black cloak making a swishing sound. He takes my hand, pulling me toward him. "Come with me."

We walk at a hurried pace away from the cemetery but to where, I'm not sure. I look up to the sky, the same sky where I heard all the horrific sounds while pinned underneath the Watchman just moments ago. There are no strange mythical creatures up there. The sky is black, almost too black, and the stars actually seem less bright. I stumble, but Zack catches my fall. It's hard to see where we're going but I can tell it's not toward the woods. I hear him murmur something, then a white light engulfs me, so bright I have to close my eyes. It only lasts a second or two but when it's gone, I'm standing next to my car and dizzy as hell.

What the...

"Get in, I'll drive," he says, opening the driver's side door as I slump against the car, trying to stop my world from spinning.

I manage to pull on the handle, opening the door and awkwardly slipping into the passenger seat. Thankfully, within seconds, the spinning begins to slow down. "Where are we going?" I ask, turning to get a better look at him. His hair is a lighter brown and way longer than I remember, and his cloak, while similar to the Watchman's, doesn't look like it's been through a bloody battle.

"Somewhere safe," he answers, driving like a bat out of hell through the cemetery gates.

Questions swirl in my head with dizzying speed. I have no choice but to let them loose.

"Where's the Watchman? Is someone trying to kill him? Where, I mean, how did he disappear when you waved your hand at him?" I rattle off, taking a breath while I watch his face contort. Apparently my questions are painful.

"I wish you didn't have to be involved in this," he whispers.

"Dammit, Zack! What the hell is going on?"

He whips to face me, his new blue eyes locking with mine. "I am not the same Zack you think I am!"

"Yeah, I can see that. But I still don't..." I stop and look away because it's weird to see my brother looking so different. "I don't understand!" I shout. "None of this makes sense!"

"The fire...the one I died in." He pauses. "I was murdered by the same people who killed Mom and Dad. Only our parents didn't come back."

"Hang on, are you saying Mom and Dad were murdered?

"I'm saying we were all targeted. And now they know about you..."

"What are you talking about? Who *know* about me?" I scream as we careen around a corner. I don't know why Zack keeps driving like someone's chasing us.

"Katie," he says in an impossibly calm tone, "the less you know, the better."

My mood instantly shifts. It's as if a switch goes off in my head. I'm no longer freaked out that my back-from-the-dead brother is driving like a lunatic in a speeding Volvo. Anger is practically boiling its way out of every pore in my body. I don't care what he does or how angry he might get, because if I don't get some answers immediately, I'm going to completely lose my shit.

"Answer me, dammit!" I scream again but he just keeps driving, barely giving me any sign that he's even listening.

I grasp my seatbelt, pushing on the latch to unlock it, watching as it slides up my shoulder and back into place. Zack is so focused on the road I'm pretty sure he doesn't even see what I'm doing. I pull up on the handle and the door swings violently open, deafening gusts of air pulsating all around us.

"What are you doing?!" he shouts, grabbing my arm as I pretend to escape.

"Tell me now!" I demand, calling his bluff. "What the *fuck* is going on?!" I scream so loudly my voice cracks.

We lock eyes and I finally see some semblance of my brother behind all the blue. He jerks his head back to the road, still tightly grasping my arm. Several black shadows flash in front of us. Zack hits the breaks, shooting me off the seat, but somehow his arm stops my body from crashing into the dash. My hand goes to my chest from the pain but I don't have time to wrap my brain around any of it. The shock that I should probably be dead right now is the only thing I can focus on before I'm pushed back against the seat.

"Close the door!" Zack shouts again, clearly enraged, so I do what he asks and yank it shut.

Nothing like almost bursting through a windshield to get someone's full attention.

He looks back to the road, shifting his head from left to right as if he's looking for something. He closes his eyes for a second, his brow furrowing in concentration, and hits the gas, turning abruptly into a dense forest. I'm not sure why I'm surprised by anything at this point but I can't help but watch in complete amazement as twigs, bushes, and small trees impossibly move away, allowing us to easily pass.

We're less than a mile into the forest when the headlights shine on something dark and huge, standing right in front of the car.

Wait...it's him—the Watchman.

Where the hell did he come from? And how in the effing world did he find us?

GRAVEYARD WATCHMAN

His large figure moves toward us in a single, fluid motion, and before I know it, I'm wrapped in another warm white light.

CHAPTER TWELVE

I OPEN MY EYES at the sound of a familiar voice. I'm lying on something hard and uncomfortable. I know the Watchman is here, but I can't make him out as I scan the area, trying to focus past the dim light surrounding me. It's impossible to see more than a few feet and when I try to pull myself up, it hurts like hell. Even taking a full breath is excruciating.

My vision is fuzzy and I'm wrapped in what feels like thick wool. It's tight around my body and I try once again to pull up. The pain keeps me from going any further and I have to catch my breath to stop from crying out.

Dear God, am I dying? Am I dead?

Suddenly, everything comes rushing back.

Zack kept me from slamming through the car windshield. At the time I felt no pain, but that has to be it.

"We have to send her back, Master," the Watchman says. "If she is captured, they will kill her!" He stops, as if just realizing his words are echoing. His voice goes into a whisper, "I cannot bear that."

Wait...did he just call my brother, "Master?"

Carefully shifting slightly to the right, I manage to catch a glimpse of firelight in my periphery and turn my head to see a flickering torch anchored on the wall.

I'm back in the cave.

"No, we have to tell her, Dominic," Zack whispers back, his tone almost defeated.

"You can make her forget," the Watchman clips back.

I can see them now. Zack's back is to me and all I can make out of the Watchman is the side of his face. I don't want either of them to know I'm awake so I stay quiet, hoping they'll continue talking.

"It's too late for that; she's hurt," Zack replies, turning his head toward me. "You know I can't do both."

I quickly shut my eyes, trying to stay as still as possible, even though my chest hurts like a mother.

"You realize she is bleeding internally," the Watchman murmurs.

"Yes." Zack's head drops down. "How many crystals are left?"

"Six."

"Take care of her. And do it quickly."

Without a word, the Watchman rises to his feet and walks in my direction. Keeping my eyes shut, I try to stay calm, sneaking peeks through the slits of my lids as he approaches. He stops only inches away from me and I can smell his earthy, masculine skin.

"Don't move her," Zack calls to him, but he doesn't reply.

Out of nowhere, a bright light illuminates through my eyelids as warm hands gently press down on either side of my shoulders. An intense, almost hot sensation envelops my body, like how the heat of the sun hits you when you walk out of an over-chilled room. The sensation is incredible and only lasts for a few seconds while pulses of what feels like small electric shocks rub in circles all over my ribcage. I have to fight to stay still, but at least it's no longer painful to breathe.

"It is done, Master."

"Excellent. Bring her to me..."

The Watchman's hands slip underneath the small of my back and behind my knees, effortlessly lifting me to his chest. I can't help but lean my head against him and wrap my hand around his warm, thick neck. His breath catches and I look up. I'm met with deep brownish-yellow eyes and if I weren't so focused on them, I'd swear we just had a moment.

He turns around and I have to hold on because the power behind his stride shifts my body. I'm waiting for the pain to return; I almost forgot that it's completely gone. My brain hasn't caught up with that fact yet. Somehow I've actually been healed and my heart starts to race in my chest.

Did that just happen? Should I be scared?

As if he can read my thoughts, he cradles me closer. I'm not sure if he thinks I'm going fight him and try to escape or if he knows I'm confused as hell right now. The warmth of his body next to mine and the familiar scent of his skin begin to calm my nerves and when I look to my left, I see Zack, standing next to a huge rock. The same rock the Watchman kneeled next to the first time I came. Only now it's glowing a soft white and I think I hear a humming sound.

We get closer and the Watchman stops, easing me to the floor but not letting go until he's sure I'm steady on my feet. I look up when his hands finally pull away. His black hood is already up as he stands stoically next to me, ignoring the intimacy we just shared. Or the intimacy I *thought* we shared.

"How do you feel?" Zack asks, stepping toward me with his hands out. I take them, noticing the warmth of them, but something is off. Somehow they don't feel solid.

"I know you have questions," he begins. "And I will answer them. But first, I need to get you home."

"Master," the Watchman interrupts.

"Dominic, she can't stay. Not yet. I need to make preparations." He looks down at my hands. "She's not like us."

Dominic nods and I have to force myself to ignore the fact that he just used that word again to identify my brother. "Tell me now!" I demand. "I don't want to go home! I don't even *have* a home anymore!"

"You must trust me, Katie," Zack says, his voice low and soothing as he gazes at me with his crazy new blue eyes.

For some reason I want to do as he says and decide to stop with the arguing. "Okay," I answer, still holding his gaze.

"Dominic, take her back like we discussed. And make it quick."

I feel a hand on my shoulder. The Watchman's hands slip underneath me, cradling me in his arms once again. His intoxicating scent of musk and masculinity surrounds me and I can't think of anything else.

"Close your eyes," the Watchman says before a web of white light shrouds us both.

Everything happens so quickly and when the white light fades, my body is instantly released from the Watchman's arms. I open my eyes and incredibly, I'm standing next to the Volvo. I look up at him and I can tell he already knows what's about to come out of my mouth.

"How in the *hell* did you do that?"

He looks down, like he doesn't know how to tell me, then shifts his eyes back to mine. "You have not lost any time."

"Huh?"

"The time. It is back to when you first arrived," he answers.

"Wait." My hand goes up. "What the hell is going on?" I ask, staring up at him.

"Now, you will not be missed." He doesn't offer any more information.

"What do you mean, I won't be missed?"

The Watchman's eyes shift away and for a second I see a hint of the familiar red. "It is not for me to explain," he answers, looking back to me, but I can hear the hesitation in his voice.

He wants me to know.

"I don't care who the hell explains it—any of it. This beating around the bush shit is driving me insane. Or maybe I've completely lost my mind and this is a flipping nightmare!"

"This is not a dream," he answers matter-of-factly.

"Then what is it? Who are you and why are you calling my dead brother 'Master'?" I air-quote the last part. "Holy shit, I sound like a mad person even to myself!" I lean against the car, almost tripping on a rock before righting myself.

The Watchman gets close, bringing his hands to my sides, and I can smell his skin again. The same masculine scent mixed with something else. It reminds me of how the north breeze smells when fall begins to push away the hot, humid summer air. It's intoxicating.

"That!" I shout, making him stand back. "Why did you do that?"

"I do not understand."

"Why are you treating me like a freaking porcelain doll?"

"I have already told you. I am your Watchman."

I can't help but roll my eyes. I know that much. "Yeah, you've told me it several times. But why? Why do you have to watch me?"

"Because you and the Master have the same bloodline," he answers in his deep, rich voice.

"Okay, I get it. He's my brother, so of course we have the same bloodline. What does that have to do with anything?"

He hesitates again, looking around as if we're being watched, then he steps closer and leans into my ear. "It means you are not of this world and must be protected."

"Not of this world? Seriously? Um, in case you haven't noticed, I'm a living, breathing person here." I don't try to hide my sarcasm but he doesn't say a word. "You're really not going to tell me, are you?"

"It is not for me to say," he says softly. "I am your protector. That is all."

"Then why am I so drawn to you?" I ask so quickly I barely realize I've said it.

His eyes dart to mine. Clearly, he wasn't expecting that. Is it wrong somehow? Wrong for me to feel this way?

He continues to glare at me but I can see the confusion behind his eyes. He's definitely baffled by this. So, I ask the next question.

"Why can't I be attracted to yo—"

"It is forbidden!" he shouts, interrupting me, and I flinch. He backs away.

"Why is it forbidden?" I ask, looking down at my feet, feeling foolish for even admitting my attraction to him.

His hand goes to my chin and our eyes lock once again. He knows I feel ashamed and probably wants to let me down gently. "It is not that simple, Kate Bassett. We are different, you and I. We are very different."

CHAPTER THIRTEEN

"Go back to the motel, Kate." He reaches around me and opens the driver's side door.

I know he's not going to elaborate because he's practically shoving me in the car, but I can't stop myself. "Wait, if you're my protector, why are you letting me drive alone? Hell, why are you letting me do anything alone?"

His lips curl up slowly, as if he's genuinely amused. "You are never alone."

I shoot up my arm so he can't shut the door. "What? Do you magically appear in my bedroom or something?"

I meet his gaze, watching the slight smile he had only seconds ago completely fade. "I am everywhere you are."

Gulp.

Our eyes stay glued for another second; he looks away first. I'm still trying to grasp what he just said when I hear a faint scream. Or maybe it was a high-pitched growl, I can't be sure. Whatever it was now has the Watchman's full attention. He pushes my shoulder all the way inside the car and slams the door, then disappears right in front of me.

Disappears.

Into thin air.

My hands shake as I try to start the engine. Light from the console catches my eye and when I look down I see it's my iPhone, in the same place I left it. It's a text from Skylar, asking where I am.

Wait, Skylar and I already had this conversation.

Oh.

My.

God.

I tap the toggle and see that it's 2:16 in the morning. The exact same moment he originally sent the text. Or I should say, the only time. The Watchman told me that time would somehow be back to normal. Clearly, I dismissed it, or more likely, I didn't believe it. Until now.

Shifting into drive, I hit the gas a little harder than intended. Gravel tumbles underneath the tires, keeping me from moving for a second before the Volvo takes off. I manage to turn around, easing up on the gas and finally hitting pavement to pass the cemetery gates. It's still pitch black outside but I'm beyond positive it shouldn't be. I've been gone for hours.

This is insane. Nothing makes sense.

The Watchman.

My dead brother—at least I think it's him—back from the dead.

Things vanishing before my eyes and now this, time standing still. Or I should say, reversing.

How can any of this be real?

What's even more insane is I'm no closer to understanding any of it. And why is that? Why are they keeping me from the truth? Zack said he was targeted. Hell, even said that our parents were too. But why? By who? Last time I checked none of us has superpowers. The Watchman talked about me having my brother's bloodline. But isn't that kind of obvious?

65

In what seems like seconds instead of minutes, I'm turning into the Holiday Inn parking lot and sure enough, it looks exactly the way it did when I left.

The lighting, the cars, the night sky.

I pull into the same parking space as an intense, warm sensation floods my body. I turn off the engine and I catch something black out of the corner of my eye. I know exactly who it is.

The Watchman.

Incredibly, I actually felt him before I saw him and now I have no doubt he can feel it too.

This is crazy.

Tapping the key fob, I hear the car doors lock as I sprint up the stairs to my room. I know the Watchman's eyes are on me but I've never been able to feel him until now. The only place I've ever seen him is at the cemetery, except when the house was on fire. Is it because I'm becoming more aware of him, or did something change? I definitely feel different, even safer somehow, especially knowing someone else or maybe, some *thing* else is after me, which is a huge relief after everything that's happened. Or wait, a few things that now haven't. The Watchman even changed that too. Hours of my life have been wiped away and I'm having a hard time wrapping my brain around all of it. Surreal doesn't even cover it because this seems way more like a dream. A crazy, scary, and yes, somewhat amazing dream.

I push the door open, closing it as quickly as I can before attaching the chain lock. Which is funny, because I know it'll work on everyone *but* him.

The Watchman disappeared right in front of me and a stupid little chain isn't going to stop him. I'm sure of that now. I'm sure of a lot of things I never thought were even possible. What he can do defies all comprehension and reasoning, and just thinking about it frightens me.

I need to refocus and somehow shut off my brain. I've been so consumed by the chaos, the Watchman, and the impossible. I'm pretty sure my mind is beginning to unravel. Yet, had I not witnessed the insanity of it all with my own eyes, I'd laugh at the person trying to convince me otherwise.

My mouth is dry and when I try to swallow I realize I'm thirsty as hell. It feels like days since I've eaten a proper meal and the more I think about it, the hungrier I get. Before I do anything I have to shower and wash away some of the madness. Then I'll check out the mini bar. Yes, eating and drinking sound fantastic right now.

I'm practically blinded by the brightness of the sterile motel bathroom and slam my foot against the small empty trash can with a curse.

Holy crap, where do they buy these ridiculously intense bulbs?

I keep my hand under the flow until the water gets warm. The tiny rivers soothe my mind as they stream down my skin. I need to keep it together and stop obsessing over everything.

For now anyway.

CHAPTER FOURTEEN

AFTER A QUICK blow dry, I pull my hair into a messy bun and slip on the fluffy white robe I left hanging behind the bathroom door. I'm too lazy to rummage through the washed, yet slightly smoke-infested clothes the neighbors managed to salvage for a pair of pajamas, so this will have to do.

The mini-fridge turns out to be nothing but a stack of protein bars and assorted soft drinks. Not exactly what I had in mind for dinner, but definitely better than nothing. Aunt Kelly's meatloaf sounds pretty fantastic right now. Grabbing two bars and a Diet Coke, I take a seat in a chair next to the tiny table and pick up my phone. No new text messages except for the one from Skylar I haven't answered yet—the one asking if I'm okay. I don't want to send him a reply and get stuck texting for ten minutes like before.

Wait. I can change what happens. Today is a half-day at school because of Thanksgiving break. Skylar and I have already had that conversation. Well, he hasn't yet, and never will now. Shit, this is weird, but could be pretty helpful in the future.

I devour the first protein bar in only three bites. The more I chew, the hungrier I get and now I understand why they call tiny foods an appetizer. This little bar would definitely be classified as one.

My phone starts to chirp and I look down, realizing it's at 10% power so I reach over and plug in the charger. After the second protein bar, I feel less confused and shaky. Probably not a bad thing since I'll most likely be processing what I should do next. Should I go back to the cemetery and find Zack? He knows I want answers. Thoughts of the Watchman instantly pop back in my head. Not my parents, or even Aunt Kelly and Uncle John. Is it because I can feel him close by? Could we have formed some kind of bond, or is it in my head? I'm clearly attracted to him and now even *he* knows that.

God, why did I tell him? Could I humiliate myself a little more?

His reaction was strange, like he couldn't, or maybe didn't, want to believe me. I know he wasn't expecting it, that's for sure. I mean, he can't be much older than me—maybe three to five years at the very max. And he admitted something else that was weird. He said, "It's forbidden." What's forbidden? Is dating frowned upon or something? I know he's not exactly like the guys I talk to at school. Hell, he's nothing like anyone I've ever met, but why did he give me that repulsed look? Is he so disgusted by me? The first guy I've liked in what feels like forever and he can't stand the sight of me.

After another few minutes of serious contemplation and self-doubt, I finally convince myself to stop obsessing about the Watchman because I can barely keep my eyes open. I'm beyond exhausted and need go to get some sleep. Besides, the mental escape is something I'm looking forward to. If I can actually fall asleep and stay asleep, maybe I'll just stay in bed for a couple of days.

Silencing my phone, I leave it face down on the table to charge. I pull back the covers, turning off the lamp before slipping in. I'm still wearing the robe because it's cold as hell in here, but that's how I like it. I hate being hot; I haven't even turned the on heater in the room. Lately I sleep way better when I can feel the weight of blankets over me. Tonight is no exception. Everything will look better tomorrow.

It has to.

§

I awaken to sunlight streaming in from the window and glance around the room, not entirely sure where I am. Oh yeah, a motel room with an adjoining door to Aunt Kelly and Uncle John's room. The same motel we're staying at because our house was completely destroyed by a fire. I have no doubt it's going take a while to figure out what our next move will be. It's like life has sucker punched each of us in the gut. Uncle John almost lost his life. Not that I would have been overly devastated, since he's an asshole, but I don't want him to die. I'm also not sure how much more Aunt Kelly can take. She's always been strong, especially when Zack and I needed her after Mom and Dad died. But now, when I look at her, I see a frail, thirty-five-year-old woman who, in the past ten years, buried her sister, brother-in-law, nephew, and son. She seriously can't take much more so I'll have to keep everything a secret. The Watchman, Zack, the crazy, unbelievable things I can't explain—all of it. I refuse to cause her any more stress. I care about her too much.

It's already 8:30. Crap, I didn't mean to sleep this late.

Pushing back the covers so quickly to get to the table, I grab my phone, nearly tripping when I reach for it. Four missed calls and seven new text messages.

Shit.

Three from Skylar and four from Aunt Kelly.

Aunt Kelly: Morning. I'm grabbing breakfast for John and me. U hungry?

My stomach begins to rumble the second my thumbs start typing back, "Starving."

Almost immediately the three dots appear—she's texting.

Aunt Kelly: I'm at Mickey D's. Want pancakes?

Me: Yes. And hash browns. TY.

Aunt Kelly: K. Be back in ten.

I smile because it feels good to have some semblance of my normal, boring life back. Even for a little while. No more insanity. No more uncertainty. Hell, could it have all just been a bad dream? Or a very vivid nightmare? I'd love to think so, but when I look down at Skylar's messages I know none of it was a dream. Needles poke at my stomach and suddenly I'm no longer hungry.

CHAPTER FIFTEEN

AFTER THROWING ON a pair of skinny jeans and my favorite gray sweater, I brush my teeth and apply a few swipes of mascara and lip gloss. I run a quick brush through my wavy hair because I let it dry against a pillow. I'm about as presentable as I'm going be today. Unfortunately, even after several hours of sleep I'm still mentally exhausted. I should probably talk my stomach into eating. I know that's part of my problem.

I grab my phone, shoving it in my back pocket as three quick knocks come from the other side of Aunt Kelly's door.

"Kate? I have your food," she says in a loud whisper.

I unlock the deadbolt and pull open the door. The smile on her face is the first thing I see, but I can tell there's worry behind her eyes. Uncle John, the house burning down, and what the hell to do next—it's got to be weighing on her. Hell, if she knew that I have an otherworldly bodyguard watching my every move, it might actually help her stress level. Wherever he is right now. The thought of him excites me but scares the crap out of me, too. Hell, I sound like some kind of psycho, even to myself.

I take the bag and drink from her hands, trying to do my best to shake off thinking about him for at least the next few minutes. "It smells great. Thanks."

"You're welcome," she says, walking through the door. "Um, weren't you supposed to be at school today?"

Shit.

"Oh, yeah. But it was a half day before Thanksgiving break, so I figured I'd sleep in."

She sighs and looks up at me. "Okay, but next time you decide not to go to school, let me know." Her tone quickly changes. "They called, asking where you were. It scared the shit out of me, Kate. And when I couldn't reach you on your phone…"

Hell, that didn't even cross my mind. I was too busy thinking about being trapped under an enormous dude in a black cloak, hovering over me while some kind of flying monster was apparently trying to kill him or me. I'm not even freaking sure anymore.

"Yeah, it kind of slipped my mind," I admit, placing the food on the tiny table and taking a seat. "I was charging my phone and forgot to turn the sound on."

"Everything okay?" she asks, pulling out a chair next to me.

Crap. She wants to talk.

"Yeah. I mean, the fire pretty much sucked." I look down because I hate lying to her. "I think I'm still kind of freaked out, that's all," I say, hoping she'll buy it. I can't exactly tell her what's *really* going on.

"I'm sure you are." Her expression changes as she cocks her head. "Dear God, is—is that Zack's necklace?"

Oh, fuck. I put it on so I wouldn't lose it.

Her eyes go wide. "Kate, what the hell is going on? How in the name of all that is holy do you have his necklace?"

I'm at a loss for words. Aunt Kelly is glaring at me like I'm insane and I'm starting to believe I am. Maybe everything that happened with the Watchman and Zack and the flying monsters is really all in my head? Could I have blacked out somehow? I've been heartbroken for so long, could I have lost my shit and actually dug up my dead brother? Am I that far gone?

Just the thought of it frightens me and I immediately feel like throwing up. I don't have an explanation. I wasn't prepared for this.

"Kate! Answer me!" she screams, startling me out of my thoughts.

A tear drops down my cheek. I don't have a choice, I have to tell her.

"Zack's not dead." I whisper the truth and watch her brows pinch together.

She reaches for my arm. "What are you talking about?"

"He's not dead, Aunt Kelly. I've seen him." I pause and watch her face change from confusion to shock. "I've talked to him, too."

She scoots back in her chair and walks over to the window, crossing her arms as she looks out at the courtyard. "Oh, yeah? Where?" she asks, humoring me.

"What do you mean?"

She turns to look me in the eyes. "Where did you see him?" she asks again, only this time, she's eerily calm

"I don't know, I—I've seen him a few times," I admit, waiting for another question but she stays quiet, so I keep going. "The first time I was taken to him," I say, watching her head tilt to the side like she's gauging my sanity.

"Who took you?"

Is she really curious or is she just gathering mental notes for a new shrink?

74

"Um, I'm not sure how to describe him other than saying he was a large man and he was wearing a black cloak."

She shakes her head slightly and smiles. "So you're telling me that some dude in a black coat took you to your dead brother?"

Her sarcasm would have pissed me off under any other circumstance, but when I hear how crazy it sounds out loud, I can't really blame her.

"I'm telling you the truth, Aunt Kelly!" I blurt out. She's the last person I want to upset. I won't lie to her anymore.

"Dammit, Kate, you've been going to that fucking cemetery for months." She pauses and walks toward me. "Even when I tried like hell to stop you, I knew you still went. There's no telling how many lies you've told me! And quite honestly, I think you've finally lost it."

Okay, now I'm pissed.

"You have no idea what I've been going through! None!" I shove my chair back and stand. "You're right, I have been going there. Even when I told you I wasn't—because grief and hopelessness were beginning to unravel everything I knew about myself!" I shout. "But no matter how many times I went or how long I forced myself to wait between visits, the same man in the same black cloak was always there. And three days ago, when it was cloudy and I thought I'd reached my limit on simply being alive at all, he looked at me. He'd never done that before. So when he walked away, I followed him. He wanted me to. I could feel it!" I stop and wipe the stupid tears now drenching my cheeks with the back of my hand.

Aunt Kelly just stares at me, flabbergasted, like if she could dial the number to the nuthouse this very minute, she would. But then she says something I don't expect.

"Holy shit." Her voice is almost trance-like. "It's happening. It's really happening."

CHAPTER SIXTEEN

MY EYES DART to hers and it's as if I'm meeting my Aunt Kelly for the first time. Is it possible she knew something about Zack's death? Our parents? And if so, how could she even fathom keeping it a secret? She knew I was desperately trying to dig my way out of a deep, horrific abyss. Simply labeling it depression doesn't cover it—not even close. If she had any information that might have helped me, even a little, why the hell wouldn't she have told me? Thoughts of how my life could have been better for months—hell, even years—flood my mind and I'm so angry I barely hear the words I scream at her.

"You knew?!" I practically charge at her, stopping only inches away. "You knew?!" I yell again, because they're the only words I can think to get out.

She flinches and closes her eyes and that's when I know for sure. She knew all along.

"Wait." She puts her hand up, as if doing so will calm me down. "I didn't know, Kate!" she shouts as tears well up in her eyes. "Not for sure, anyway."

For a second, I want to hug her, because that's what I always do. I don't want to see her upset and I always do everything I can to keep her from worrying about me. But now I'm starting to doubt everything I know about her. Clearly, I've been the fool all along about Zack, my parents—even her and Uncle John. It's no secret they've had money problems for years and they were all too happy to take me in when Zack died. I had a huge inheritance. And that's when it hits me—my reality is starting to become crystal clear and the anger is back with a vengeance.

"Not for sure?!" I shout sarcastically. I watch tears stream down her cheeks but I don't give a shit—I'm beyond pissed.

"Calm down, Kate! It's not that simple!"

She touches my arm but I yank it back and walk away. I barely want to be in the same room with her.

"Will you *please* sit down?" she asks, her voice draped in worry. The same worry I've been trying so hard to prevent before today. It pulls at my heartstrings; I'm pretty sure she knew it would.

"Come on, Kate," her brows push together, "you can at least give me that much."

Cheap shot, but I decide to do what she asks—for now. Nodding my head, I follow her to the table and take a seat. I'm fully aware that my body is trembling, but I'm not sure if it's because I'm still furious with her or frightened that my world is falling apart. Lacing my fingers together to stop the shaking, I wait for her to start. But first, she pulls a couple of tissues out of the complementary box sitting in the middle of the table and takes a deep breath. I don't say a word. I need the truth. I need her to tell me everything.

She shifts in her chair before locking eyes with me. "Do you remember your grandfather, William?"

I'm a little confused by her question. She knows how close we were, he was her and my mother's father. But why is she bringing him up?

"Of course I remember him." I pause because it almost feels like she's changing the subject. "What does Papa have to do with all of this?"

Aunt Kelly takes another deep breath and closes her eyes as she exhales. "He didn't...he didn't die of a heart attack like everyone thinks." She stops and puts her hand to her chest with a sigh, like admitting it was a huge relief, but I can hear the struggle in her voice.

I wait a few more seconds in the silence as she wipes at the corner of her left eye. "Okay, so, he didn't die of a heart attack." I repeat her words, still totally confused why we're even discussing this right now.

I was ten when Papa died; he was the first person I lost who meant everything to me. He taught me how to fence because it was his passion. We would spend hours discussing strategies and practicing how to take control in impossible situations. I came to love the sport and even went on to compete, but it wasn't the same without him. Until the fire, I still had my sabre and protective gear. I couldn't part with any of it because they were all gifts from him. Now they're gone forever. All those memories.

None of it explains why she brought him up, though. "What does any of this have to do with Papa? He's been gone for years."

Aunt Kelly locks eyes with me and says, "It has everything to do with him because he died saving your life."

Wait, what?

I'm not sure how to respond or even what to say. I'm completely taken off guard and it feels like I've been gut punched. Hard. There's no way he died saving me. I wasn't even there.

"Huh? How is that possible? I wasn't with him when he died," I say as tiny pieces of that day begin jarring something vaguely familiar in the back of my mind. I shift in my chair to keep fresh needles from poking at my gut.

"Oh, you were there, you just don't remember." She takes my hand and this time, I don't stop her. I'm pretty sure she knows I'm starting to lose it. "The blow to your head was pretty severe, honey. It was even touch and go with you for a while there. And, according to the doctors, you'll probably never regain full memory of that day." She stops and squeezes a little harder. "But it's also possible it could all come flooding back. The brain is tricky like that."

"What happened?" I ask, even more confused than before.

"I don't know, Kate, no one does. You were the only one with him when he died."

Oh.

My.

God.

I'm trying to process this new information when Aunt Kelly says, "You were unconscious when they found you." She scoots her chair closer to me.

"When who found me?" I ask, trying to will away the nausea creeping its way into my stomach.

"Zack," she admits, "and your dad."

"If Papa and I were alone, how did Dad and Zack know where we were?"

"Oh, he always made sure your parents knew where you two practiced," she explains. "Especially Zack."

"Why?" I ask. This is getting more confusing by the second.

Aunt Kelly looks away and exhales before her eyes return to mine. "It's time you knew the truth," she begins, her voice getting more intense. "Our lineage goes back nearly a thousand years. Your mom and me, Zack, and now you."

What the hell is she bringing this up for? I already know our family goes back to some dude named William the Conqueror.

"Yeah, Mom showed me the family tree years ago. But what does this have to do with—"

"It has everything to do with what's going on now."

Holy shit, she's serious.

"Okay, but I still don't get why."

"Kate, you've been given hints about this your entire life, and, to be fair, we—I mean, your parents and I—didn't think it would even affect you. Hell, it's been dormant for decades." She looks away as if she's replaying something in her mind. "Well, until Meredith and Adam were killed." Her voice cracks a little when she says my mom and dad's names.

I choke back a sob. "Zack told me that they were targeted."

"He's right," she responds, taking another tissue. "They were killed by..." She stops again, like it's hard to get the words out.

"Tell me!" I demand, swallowing back the new lump in my throat.

She shakes her head, "You're going think it's crazy. Jesus, even I think it's crazy."

"Just say it!" I shout a little louder than intended.

Aunt Kelly closes her eyes for a moment, like she's debating whether to go further. My body is starting to tremble again and I know she can feel it. Out of the blue, she blurts out, "They were killed by Earth Demons."

What the hell did she just say?

"Come again?" I say, not even trying to mask my disbelief.

"It's true, Kate, and just because you don't believe it right now doesn't mean it isn't real." She clears her throat. "You and I, and Zack, are..." She stops again and takes another deep breath. "You and Zack and I are all part of the Order of the Celestial Hierarchy."

"Huh?" is all I get out because I have no words. She's clearly lost her freaking mind. I mean, what the hell does *Celestial Hierarchy* even mean? I'm literally trying to Google my brain for more information when she takes both of my hands, squeezing them as if bracing me for the worst.

"You, my dear, are half Seraph."

CHAPTER SEVENTEEN

AUNT KELLY SMILES like she just gave me good news and her eyes well up again. She reaches for another tissue; I can do nothing but stare. I don't even know what to say or hell, what to think. I have no idea what she's talking about.

"Okay, first of all, what the hell is a Seraph? And if you actually believe any of this is really happening, how the hell did I not know about it?"

Her face drops and she scowls, like she knows I'm not buying it.

"I mean, I know *you* believe it, Aunt Kelly, but..."

"Kate," she stops me, her expression now much more serious, "listen to me very carefully. Seraph is the proper noun that refers to the word Angel," she says matter-of-factly, shifting in her chair, "and that necklace you're wearing is proof that your brother, my nephew, is no longer in his coffin. If you can accept that he's actually alive, then why the hell can't you believe what I'm trying to tell you?"

Whoa. She's got a point.

"Okay, say I believe you," I begin, "and everything you've been telling me is real. That still doesn't explain how I've gone my whole life without knowing. I mean, wouldn't I feel different if I'm supposed to be, I don't know, *different?*"

"You didn't know because we, meaning, all of us—your mom, your dad, even Zack—thought it was over. We thought the line was dormant. There was no indication that any of us would carry the line further." She pauses and looks away before locking eyes with me again. "That is, until now. And you're not necessarily different, you just have abilities you haven't tapped into yet."

"Abilities? I have untapped abilities? What kind?" I ask, hoping I'm not going to turn into some kind of freak monster.

"I don't know, honey. Zack didn't know his abilities either. But now..." She bites one side of her lip. "I'm pretty sure if he came back from the dead he's a Seraph Master."

"Master! Yes, I've heard the Watchman call him that!"

Okay, now we're getting somewhere.

"Watchman?" Aunt Kelly repeats.

"Yeah, he was always at the cemetery when I was there to visit Zack's grave. I followed him one day..." I'm not sure how much I should tell her. "I eventually found Zack."

She tilts her head and I can almost see her wheels spinning. "Wait a second." She blinks like she's putting the puzzle pieces together. "Did you say he was wearing a black cloak?"

"Yes!" I answer, happy to finally be telling someone about this.

Her eyes drift off and she lets out a breath. "Then that means the battle might have already begun..."

"What battle?"

Aunt Kelly's face drops; she looks off in the distance and I can tell she's miles away, reliving a memory. I knock on the table and she snaps out of it, locking eyes with me.

"Do you still remember what Papa taught you?" she asks with renewed excitement.

I know what she's talking about, but why is she changing the subject? "Y-yeah, I think so. Why?"

She laughs. "Are you kidding? He spent years teaching you how to fence. Do you think that was a coincidence?"

Holy crap, is she saying what I think she's saying?

"Hold on!" My hand automatically goes up. "You're not suggesting I can fight those...those whatever those things are that the Watchman protected me from—are you?"

Her eyes go big and I remember I haven't told her about that part yet.

"You've already been attacked?" she whispers, her expression shrouded in shock.

I look away for a second, slightly embarrassed. "I...I think so. I mean, I didn't see anything—I couldn't. The Watchman had me covered with his cloak. But I could hear what sounded like flapping wings and..." I trail off because this part is ridiculous, even to me.

"Go on," Aunt Kelly insists.

"I know it sounds crazy, but..."

"Fire. You heard fire, didn't you?" she says, nodding her head.

Jesus, how does she know all this?

"Yes."

I watch her scoot back from her chair and slowly walk to the window. She pushes her brown hair away from her face and stands, looking out as if in a sudden daydream.

"What? Tell me..." I plead, hoping she's not going to drop another bombshell, but she only continues to stare. It feels like a full ten minutes go by before she turns back to me.

"It was an Earth Demon."

My stomach knots up at the word "Demon." Demons are imaginary. They aren't real.

"How badly was he hurt?" she asks and I know she's talking about the Watchman.

"Pretty badly. I mean, his back was ripped to shreds and then Zack showed up out of nowhere." I can tell by her expression she's waiting for me to keep going. "He helped the Watchman walk a few steps before telling him to 'take a crystal.'" I air-quote the last three words.

"Do you know if this Watchman has had to take any other crystals?"

"Yeah, the first time I followed him." My eyes go to hers. "It was the same day as the storm and he was somehow hurt." I swallow. "Again, he had me in his cloak so I don't know what or how it happened."

"No, that's okay. I'm just…" She trails off like she's trying to think. "That means he may only have a few crystals left."

"I don't understand. Why are these crystals so important?" I ask, trying once again to keep the pins and needles from poking around in my gut.

"Kate, those are healing crystals. They're extremely rare, so if this Watchman guy has them, he's earned them.

"Healing? Like, bringing him back to life?"

"No, they can't quite do that. As far as I know, only a Seraph Master can bring life back. And even then, only once. And, seriously, you should probably call him by his rightful title."

"Rightful title?" I repeat.

"Yes, he's a Seraph Warrior."

"The Watchman? Okay, but Zack just calls him Dominic."

Aunt Kelly shakes her head and looks back out the window. She squints when something catches her eye, trying to get a better view, and her mouth drops. She turns to me and I jump out of my chair, almost tripping on the carpet to see for myself. His black cloak waves slightly in the wind as he stands about two hundred feet away on a hill just beyond the parking lot.

"That's him!" I blurt out louder than I meant to. "That's the Watchman...I mean, Dominic." I pull my voice back to a whisper.

"Oh, I believe you," she admits. "But why is he showing himself?"

"What do you mean? I see him all the time."

"In broad daylight?"

"Well, yeah, sort of. There's usually some daylight left when I see him at the cemetery," I explain, wondering why she's even asking.

"Have you ever seen him in the early afternoon outside your motel room?"

Okay, she's got me there.

"Well, no. But I guess he's doing what he's supposed to be doing and watching out for me."

"Kate, he wouldn't be making it obvious unless he was trying to get your attention."

Shit.

"O-okay, I'll get dressed. Hang on," I say, frantically grabbing my phone as I pull my grey sweater over my head.

"Here." Aunt Kelly hands me a sneaker as I hop into my jeans.

"Thanks," I get out, rushing to the bathroom.

"Okay, he's still there," she calls to me. "it doesn't look like he's moved."

I quickly brush my teeth and apply some mascara before yanking up my shirt to swipe on deodorant, and running chapstick over my lips.

"Shit! He's gone!" Aunt Kelly whisper-shouts and I realize she's trying to keep it down because Uncle John is most likely sleeping in the other room.

I run out of the bathroom and grab my keys. "I'll drive to the cemetery," I say. "Maybe that's where he's gone."

"I'm going with you!" Aunt Kelly grabs my arm and then her face suddenly drops. I know what's going through her mind. Uncle John. She can't leave him. Not now.

"I'll be okay." I smile and give her a quick hug, "I've got a body guard now, remember?"

Her eyes already welling up. "Oh Kate. Be...be careful, honey. This isn't a game."

I smile again, trying to reassure her as I reach for the door. "I'll try to text you."

I run as fast as I can down the open hallway, practically slamming into a black shape just before making it to my car. Large hands slip around my waist and I look up to see Dominic's brownish-red eyes staring down at me. I smile at first because, if I'm being honest, I missed his smell and his touch. But before I can say a word, he swoops me into his arms and my world goes black.

Almost instantly my other senses kick in and it feels as if my body is being lifted and pulled horizontal, almost like I'm flying. Out of nowhere, gusts of wind swirl around me and I hear large wings flapping, thrusting us slightly up and down with each stroke.

Oh. My. God. This can't be happening. We can't be flying. I must be dreaming.

I'm hit with a blast of nausea and I try like hell to will the bile from creeping up my throat. No, no, no...

Calm down, Kate. You. Are. Okay. I tell myself over and over, concentrating on every word as I try to divert the overwhelming urge to hurl all over myself.

You are okay. Yes, get in a rhythm. You are okay, you are okay.

I barely have time to appreciate the relief before a hard thud to the ground pushes my body forward. I feel the Watchman's arms slip a little tighter around my waist, keeping me securely pressed up against him until we're steady and in one place. Clearly, we've landed. At least I freaking hope we have. The urge to vomit subsides now that I'm standing on my own two feet.

"Kate," he says a few seconds later, startling me out of my thoughts. He's warm, almost too warm, his scent intoxicating.

I finally open my eyes, looking up into his warm, brownish-red eyes and for the first time since I saw him five months ago, I'm not at all afraid. He's looking back at me with the same intense gaze and without thinking, I reach up and cup the right side of his face. He closes his eyes. His unshaven skin feels rough and masculine against my palm and that's when it hits me. I want him, more than I've ever wanted anything in my entire life.

"Kate," he says again, "are you able to stand on your own?"

I don't think I could answer right now if my life depended on it. Our eyes are still locked and I don't want to let go. And I sure as hell don't want him to either. Words have escaped me. I stand completely still, frozen in his embrace, hoping this moment never ends.

"We must talk," he says before gently taking my arms and guiding me to a seat. Or, I should say, a flat, cold rock.

Where are we?

It's cold, damp, and under-lit. The cave. The cold, damp, under-lit, wonderful cave.

He walks away, his hood falling back, black hair spilling around his face. After a few steps, he turns back to me. "Forgive me. I—I could not stop this from happening." He looks down and then away. "Forgive me," he says again.

I'm so mesmerized by his sheer masculine beauty I can barely breathe, but his words somehow pull me out of my revelry. "What do you mean?" I ask, genuinely confused.

He turns his gaze back to me and takes in a deep breath, as if preparing me for the worst. "I am afraid I have marked you."

CHAPTER EIGHTEEN

"MARKED?" I REPEAT, pushing up my sleeves for some sign of bruises, but there aren't any. "What are you talking about?"

The Watchman brings his hands together, raising them to his face as if he's tortured by his own guilt. The prickly sensation is back, poking around in my gut. It's almost like I'm feeling his torment.

"It means I have claimed you," he pauses, "for myself." His eyes meet mine with a new intensity.

"Claimed me?" I repeat him again because I'm not seeing a problem here. "Makes sense, I mean, Zack said you're my protect—"

"Not that kind of protector!" he interrupts and the needles prick a little harder. My hand goes immediately to my abdomen and he cringes.

"Then what? What the hell are you saying?" I ask, matching the volume of his voice as it echoes throughout the cave.

"I have chosen you." Frustration washes over his features as he stands only inches away.

"Okay, I get that…"

"For my mate!" He shouts again but this time he pulls me close, wrapping his massive arms around me.

Whoa, I wasn't expecting this—and I'm pretty sure he knows it.

I can't deny that I'm attracted to him. I knew that from pretty early on, but the idea of him being more to me than a fantasy is something entirely different. I know nothing about him, only that he makes me feel safe. But where did he come from? And what is a Seraph Warrior?

"Say something," he whispers, still holding me tightly to his chest. "Please."

The desperation in his voice hits me like a crashing wave and I regret how clueless I've been as hundreds of questions slam into my head at once. It's hard to know which one to ask first. But there's something I need know before anything else. Something he needs to explain.

He pulls back but his arms are still wrapped around my waist. I slowly lift my head and look up into the eyes of an incredibly handsome, rugged-featured young man. The wisdom behind his gaze is clear and it's getting harder to concentrate.

"I...I hardly know you," I finally get out. "How could you feel so much for me—so quickly?" I ask, trying to keep firm eye contact as I wait for him to answer.

He closes his eyes but doesn't let go. He nuzzles my neck, breathing a soft sigh before the words pour out of his mouth. "It was not Zack who sent me to watch over you, it was the Seraph Council," he admits, "I have known you longer than you realize and have been your Watchman since before you began fencing with your grandfather." He swallows and keeps going. "He knew even back then that the Seraphian battles were inevitable—he just did not know when they would happen or even if anyone would be chosen." The corners of his eyes bunch up and for the first time, I actually see his face brighten up into a slight smile.

"Me?" I whisper, still holding his gaze.

"You," he confirms.

"Chosen for what?" I ask, and my voice cracks a little.

"You are the chosen sovereign."

"Huh?" I giggle because even in my head it sounds ridiculous. "What do you mean, like a queen or something?"

He nods and when my eyes go wide I can actually see his face brighten into a genuine smile. "And please, Kate. Call me Dominic."

I can't help but smile back. I've never called him by his first name to his face. Even though I know it, he's only ever been "The Watchman" to me.

"I think I can do that," I whisper, looking up into his incredible eyes. His massive arms wrap a little tighter around my waist and suddenly, I don't care how crazy this is or that I hardly know anything about this man—because truth be told, he's captivated me from the beginning. And right now the safety and peace I feel when I'm around him is enough.

He leans down and I'm sure he's about to kiss me. An intense pulse between my legs nearly shatters me and I almost lose my breath. The closer we get the more I can smell his delicious, sultry musk mixed with sky and a touch of evergreen or rosemary—we're only inches apart and I can almost taste his masculinity.

My eyes flash open at the sound of movement behind me. I feel Dominic's body tighten; he pulls back, putting space between us.

We're not alone...

"Hello, Katie," Zack says, startling me out of the sheer bliss I know I was about to experience. "I see Dominic brought you back to me as I instructed."

Dominic loosens his hold, allowing me to turn around. Zack's timing totally sucks, I'll admit, but the second I see my brother again I don't try to stop myself and run straight into his arms.

He hugs me tightly but lets go before I'm ready and locks eyes with me, holding me steady with his hands. "You can no longer be without our full protection," he says firmly, then looks up at Dominic. "They can't know where she lives for the sake of the other family members."

Oh God, he's talking about Aunt Kelly and Uncle John.

"I agree," Dominic says, quickly glancing over to me before pulling up his hood, back to being on guard again.

My heart drops when he turns around and walks through the cave's arched opening and doesn't look back. Not even once. I want to run after him. I don't want to be apart from him ever again. I can't explain the sudden intensity, even to myself. I've never felt this way about anyone. Ever. My mind is racing but before I can fully grasp why I'm so bipolar about Dominic, Zack takes my hand.

"He has bonded with you, but do not worry. He will be back." He pauses, patting my hand. "You and Dominic are now one."

Okay, wait a second…

"Marked," I insist. "He said he marked me."

"Yes. Which means you will feel his thoughts and emotions and he will feel yours. That is why you longed for him to stay."

"H-how did you know?"

"It is how being bonded with someone works in our world," he explains. "It's all right, Katie. I could see it in your face, even in your body language."

"Wait. Are you saying we're, like…" I pause because I can't believe what I'm about to say out loud, "*married*—or something?"

Zack smiles and squeezes my hand. "Sister, this goes way beyond simple mortal marriage. You are eternal mates."

Holy.

Crap.

On.

A.

Cracker.

"What in God's name? Hold on, Zack!" My hands go up in surrender. "I'm only seventeen!" I shout, tearing up because I hate the words coming out of my mouth. I want Dominic. Badly. But this...this is too much.

"Katie, calm down. It is your destiny. You have no choice in the matter."

"But, but—" I lock eyes with him again. "I thought it... or, I mean, me dating Dominic...or shit, whatever this is, was forbidden! Last time I saw you, he specifically said 'it's forbidden!'"

Zack cocks his head and smiles slightly. "Typically it is. Seraph Warriors are not to mate with anyone who is only half Seraph."

"Why?" I ask, not sure if I want the answer.

He sighs, pushing his brows together, "Because Seraph Warriors are not human."

Gulp.

You don't need to worry, Katie." Zack tries to console me, "It's clear that your destiny was set a long time ago—you are our Seraph Sovereign now. You may mate with whomever you please."

"Seraph Sovereign?" I repeat, trying to wrap my brain around the non-human thing but also, remembering what Aunt Kelly told me. A Seraph is actually...an Angel? Yeah, that was it. I try to swallow but can't get past the dryness. "And now I'm

Dominic's mate? Can this possibly be real?" I begin to tremble, part of me hoping—no, praying—Dominic shows back up and flies me the hell out of here.

Zack must have clued in that I'm about to lose it and guides me over to the flat rock. "Sit down and breathe, Katie," he says, rubbing my shoulders as my heart pounds in my chest. "Allow me to explain."

"I'm good," I say, holding up my hand. "I'm pretty sure I don't want to know any more details of this madness."

But when I gaze back up into Zack's new blue eyes, the realization slams into my body that *this is real*. All of it is real and I can no longer pretend my life will ever be normal again.

My nervous attempt at sarcasm makes him chuckle under his breath.

"It means you have a great deal of responsibility." He walks around to face me with a smile that's too serious to fully reach his eyes.

"Okaaay." I stretch out the word trying to slow down the insanity of our conversation. "So, um, what does being the Seraph Sovereign mean—exactly?" I ask, bracing myself for more unbelievable news.

Impossibly, Zack's eyes seem more intense, like the cobalt blue is somehow swirling, accentuating the severity of what he's about to tell me. Or maybe it's just me seeing things.

All I know is I am so not ready for this.

"It means that you were chosen, this is your destiny and you must take it very seriously."

"Zack, if you don't start making sense right now..."

"You are the fifteenth female born of our ancient FitzRobert lineage," he continues, taking a seat next to me.

"Hang on," I stop him, "does this have anything to do with that William the Conqueror dude?"

"Yes," he smiles, nodding his head, "it has everything to do with him." He shifts to face me. "Some referred to him as William the Bastard because of his father's affair with a woman named Herleva. Her background and the circumstances of William's birth have always been shrouded in mystery but we're pretty sure her blood, or I should say *Seraph blood,* is what started our line."

Holy...

My hands are shaking even more than they were a moment ago. "Aunt Kelly... She said something about the line being dormant, or maybe something skipping a generation? Is that why she and Mom weren't affected?"

"That's exactly right." Zack confirms. "When William, our 31st grandfather, was knighted in his teens by King Edward the Confessor, that kickstarted his Seraph Warrior blood. Once he became the King of England, our royal ties were set in motion."

"Wow," I whisper, trying to take it all in as nausea begins to churn in my gut. "So he was a Warrior first?"

Zack nods.

"That's why I was so attracted to Dominic, even from the beginning...because I'm part Seraph, too." I try to swallow again but my mouth is still too dry.

"Yep, you're getting it." Zack stands up, walking a few steps away before turning around to face me. "As you know, we thought our Seraph line was in dormancy but after I came back, it was obvious the legacy didn't skip me or you. But in my mind, that still didn't mean any of this would involve you until I did more research. That's when I fully understood and realized that you happen to be the fifteenth FitzRobert female. The one, according to the research, who would be appointed to lead the Seraphians." He pauses. "And looking back throughout our entire lineage, the numbers work," he kneels down, "that you, my dear, are our new Queen." He bows his head.

He knelt. And bowed his head. To me. Me!

I must be having a nightmare or perhaps I just dropped dead because I can't feel my body. My limbs feel stiff and it's getting harder to breathe and all my senses have left me. Shuffling feet and what sounds like conversation surround me but I can't make out the words. My heart is still pounding, I know that much, but my fingers are cold and numb.

"Katie!" I hear my name, but it sounds like it's coming from far away and I can't move. A burst of air swirls heavily around me like there are a hundred people sprinting by.

"Dominic, take her to the castle!" the familiar voice demands. "And hurry! I think she might be in shock!"

Out of nowhere, incredible warmth engulfs me and everything goes away. It's as if I'm tightly shrouded in a fresh-out-of-the-dryer black feather comforter—it's pure heaven. Maybe I did die. Maybe this is what it feels like…and, if it is, I don't ever want it to end.

CHAPTER NINETEEN

MY EYES FLASH open, pulling me out of a terrifying dream of shadowy creatures with red, glowing eyes. I try to shake off the horrific images. I'm on a sofa or maybe a bed; something soft. I can hear whispering or maybe someone praying.

Mentally pushing away the layer of cobwebs from what feels like years of sleeping, I have to squint and refocus when I look to my right. The whispering is coming from Dominic, who is kneeling next to the bed. He looks up as if he knows I'm awake and nods once before taking a few steps back.

Did he just bow?

"How are you feeling?" he asks softly.

I'm not worried about my health as much as I'm curious where we are. The stone walls are at least two stories high, with windows reaching from floor to ceiling. Totally different than the cold, damp cave we just left.

"Where are we?" I ask, attempting to pull myself out of the bed.

"Do not try to get up. You must take it slowly," he says, coming a little closer.

My brows push together before he goes on. "You were treated for shock and have been asleep for almost ten hours."

Huh?

I let my head fall back onto a stack of pillows, shifting when something bright catches my eye. Blazing sparks fly from the biggest, most gorgeous fireplace I've ever seen. The dancing flames highlight panel after panel of heavy drapery hanging from the impossibly high ceiling, the light enhancing the rich tones of reds, golds, and purples. Between them are layers of thick rock, shining candelabras lighting up the room on either side. To my right, massively carved doors hint that there's way more beyond this.

My hands automatically spread over what looks and feels like pure silk, covering me to my waist. I'm not on just any bed or sofa. I'm in the most beautifully draped four-poster bed I've ever laid eyes on.

This is unbelievable.

I've never, ever seen anything like this and the more I think about it, the more I wonder how the hell we got to the freaking Ritz Carlton.

Dominic pulls back his hood. "You are safe but you still need rest."

"Where are we? Will I be sleeping here tonight?" I ask, watching the corners of his lips curl into a smile.

Um, did I say something funny?

He takes another step toward me and I'm captivated by his masculine stride, barely noticing that I'm holding my breath when he reaches for my hand. Even though I'm no longer frightened of him, he's still an enormous man. The warmth of his touch mixed with the smell of his skin piques an even deeper desire inside me. It's all I can do *not* to wrap my arms around his neck and pull him close.

"This is our home," he whispers.

Our home?

When he smiles again it hits me. Somehow, he knows what I'm thinking. Or at least he does right now. Didn't Zack say that the bond we share...?

Holy crap, can he actually read my thoughts or just feel my emotions?

I'm instantly embarrassed and have to look away, but Dominic takes my other hand and I automatically gaze up into his reddish-brown eyes.

"I am pleased that you desire me. I have waited so," he takes in a quick breath, "so very long for you..."

His intense stare practically drips with passion, making it clear that he means every word. I have to blink a few times to keep from getting dizzy. Zack was right. I can feel his emotions, too, and the growing pit in my stomach reminds me of it.

"Get some rest," he says, letting go of my hands.

Is he serious? I've been sleeping for hours.

"You're leaving?" I ask as calmly as I can, trying to mask how badly I want him to stay.

A small smile spreads across his lips again. "I will not be far. Your brother and I have a few things to take care of," he says in a low, hushed voice, nodding his head once before turning away.

My eyes follow his large, athletic frame as he walks out the gigantic wooden door, closing it behind him. I miss him already. It's like I have an insatiable thirst—no, hunger—for his touch. I want to be near him without interruption.

Jesus, get ahold of yourself, Kate.

An unexpected vibration from underneath me scatters my thoughts and I automatically reach for my back pocket.

No way...is that my phone?

I nearly drop it trying to get the screen to light up. Six missed calls and thirteen texts. Most of them from Aunt Kelly but a few from Skylar.

Without thinking, I hit the redial button and before it starts ringing, Aunt Kelly is on the line, already asking questions.

"Kate, where are you—are you okay?" The urgency in her voice is palpable. "Are you safe?"

"Yes, I'm okay but, I...I'm not sure." My eyes drift around the room again. Might as well tell her the truth. "I'm in some kind of fancy hotel that looks more like a freaking castle."

"Castle?" she says, and I can hear the tremor in her voice.

"What's going on? Aunt Kelly? Are you crying?" I ask, hoping I'm wrong. "I'm okay. Everything is okay."

She doesn't answer right away but I can hear her choke back tears. "It's—it's John," she finally says. "He left sometime during the night. I haven't been able to find him."

"How? What?" I blurt out. "He has second degree burns on his arm and leg and he can barely breathe without coughing." Stating the obvious doesn't actually help me try to work out this new development.

"I know," Aunt Kelly whispers in a more serious tone. "And earlier, when I took the bandages off to dress the wounds, they were..." She pauses for a second. "They were almost healed."

I try to swallow but there's a sudden lump in my throat. "That's impossible."

Something isn't right and she knows it too.

"Kate, come back, I need you," she begs, and the desperation in her voice is like a knife to my gut.

I have to go. I have to help her find him.

"Okay." I jump out of bed but have to steady myself against the bedpost to catch my balance. Dominic was right, I needed to do that way slower.

Crap.

Just the thought of him makes me desperate to stay...but I can't. Aunt Kelly needs me and has always been there when I needed her. I have no choice. I have to help her.

"Okay. I don't know how I'll get there but I'll be there as soon as I can." I hang up, trying to shake off the foreboding feeling in my chest.

CHAPTER TWENTY

THE HALLWAY IS lit with torches all the way down in each direction, beautifully enhancing the gorgeous, evenly-spaced tapestries, one after the other. The dancing light gives them an almost magical appearance, landscapes and portraits of rolling hills with white doves and people I don't recognize. I'm mesmerized by their beauty and it takes a second to shake it off. I can't lose focus now. I need to find the way out, and fast—before anyone knows I'm missing. I rush down the hallway, trying to keep calm, when a strange feeling washes over me, almost warning me to stay, but it's gone so quickly I'm not sure if it was my nerves or something else.

I'll go with nerves for now.

Picking up the pace, I run on the balls of my feet, trying to stay as quiet as possible. The hallway seems to go on forever and I'm about to devise another plan when I get to a corner. I stop to peek around, my hand automatically going to my mouth to hush my breathing. I have to stay quiet. I can't get caught now. Trying again, I see two men sitting across from each other at a candlelit table. They're talking so quietly I can't make out what they're saying. Both are dressed in cloaks similar to Dominic's, though theirs are dark brown, not pure black like his—and neither of the two men are nearly as big in stature.

I hold my breath and dart past the door, sprinting as fast as I can until I finally get to an enormous archway at the end of the hallway. It's totally black and I can only see a few feet beyond.

This doesn't look good.

My mind races with thoughts of running back to my incredible bed and burying myself under those amazing silk covers. It wouldn't take long and I know the way back. If anyone asks, I'll just say I was looking around. They'll believe me...I'm the Queen, right? I can do whatever I want.

What am I thinking?

I have to get out of here. I told Aunt Kelly I was on my way. This isn't my place. I have a life, a family—shit, I have to graduate.

Trying to gather every ounce of courage I have left, I take off in a dead run through the blackness, shivering as the air begins to change, growing thicker somehow. It's harder to take a breath and I have no choice but to slow down. The blackness surrounds me and I can't adjust my eyes enough to see anything. My heart is pounding too fast and I can feel the edges of panic creeping in. Something yanks me around the waist and before I know it, my feet are no longer on the ground. I struggle like hell to get free, twisting and turning, but it's no use. I'm trapped, uselessly gulping for air in the deafening blackness.

This can't be it—this can't be how I die...

We drop hard as light spills all around us, and I practically vacuum the oxygen into my lungs. I barely get a chance to see who's holding me before I'm lifted up into a standing position. We're back outside, on some kind of hill. I slowly look up, bracing myself for the worst. His brownish-red eyes glare down at me. I gasp, throwing a hand over my mouth.

Dominic.

Thank God.

I can't let him know how relieved I am to see him, relieved that it was him in the blackness and not some other scary *something*. But I can't fall under his spell or whatever this is between us. I can't stay here. I have to get to Aunt Kelly. I have to get back to my normal life.

"W-what the hell?" I scream, allowing my tone to seep with more hatred than I feel. "Are you to trying to save me or kill me?"

He backs away, fuming. I can tell he's beyond angry but he doesn't say a word. He just stands with his back to me, ten feet away and breathing like he just ran a marathon. Another few seconds go by before he turns around and locks eyes with me.

"You must never do that again," he shouts, still panting but not as hard as before.

"Okay, I'll never do it again," I repeat his words, not even trying to disguise my sarcasm because now I'm just pissed. He screwed up my chance to get away from this madness.

"You do not understand the severity of what just happened!"

"Severity?" I say, cocking my head as I roll my eyes.

His nostrils flare but his eyes stay glued to mine. I'm definitely striking a nerve, which is totally my intent. I don't want to sleep in a fancy room with some dude protecting me because I'm some kind of freaking Queen of the Seraphs or whatever bullshit this is. It's ridiculous, even crazy, and I'm getting the hell out of here.

"I allowed you to leave our room." His glare almost pierces through me. "I allowed you to look around, to find your bearings," he pauses for a second, "but when you ran for the Hall of Warriors…" His eyes close as if he's in physical pain. "You could have…"

He doesn't have to finish the sentence. I know the missing word.

"Well I didn't, so you can relax!" I bite out, hoping to keep him mad enough to let me go. "Look, I'm sure you can find another queen." I pause, wondering for a moment if provoking him is the best course of action. "Just Tell Zack, or whoever is in charge, that I got away—or tell the truth. I don't want to do this, any of it…"

"Another queen?" His gaze shifts from either side of me, as if checking to see if the coast is clear. "Come!" He yanks me by one arm, pulling me with such force it actually hurts.

"Ow! Stop!" I shout, but he puts his other hand over my mouth, walking me down the hill until I see the cemetery, the same familiar place I know very well.

"Do you see that gravestone?" he growls, pointing in the direction of Zack's resting place.

"Yeah. Why?" I say in my best bitch voice.

He turns me around to face him, his hands tight on my shoulders. "Because you'll be buried next to him if you do not listen to me carefully!" His words feel like they're cutting into my flesh.

He wants me to feel his anger.

"You are Seraph Queen, like it or not."

"I don't want it!" I yell, trying to stomp off, but his hands are faster and he yanks me back. "Dammit, Dominic, let me go! I can't do this! I want to go home!"

"It is not a matter of you wanting it. It is already done."

"Well, undo it!" I shout, locking eyes with him again.

"It is impossible," he says in a low, deep voice.

"Why?" My voice quivers as tears well up in my eyes. "I just don't understand. Why me?"

His face changes and his brows push together. His voice gets quieter, softer, like he knows I feel defeated. "Kate, it is your destiny, your duty." He stops, gently cupping my face in his hands as a warm sensation travels down between my legs. "As long as I still have breath left in me, I will never stop fighting for you."

I have to swallow to keep the knot from forming in my throat; I'm pretty sure he notices because his eyes drop to my mouth. I can feel his desire for me even without our unique bond. The gentle lust behind his eyes alone says it all. He wants me.

A single tear manages to escape down my cheek and his thumb catches it, wiping it away as he slowly leans down. After what seems like an eternity, he touches his lips to mine. They feel amazingly soft and warm and his tenderness takes me by surprise. My breath catches when he carefully slips an arm around my waist, pulling me closer. Without thinking, I reach around his neck as our mouths move in perfect unison. A flood of passion pulses through me. A slight hint of his gentle tongue nearly does me in and my legs begin to shake.

Or maybe it's the vibration in my back pocket.

I grab for my phone, feeling around until I touch to the top button to turn it off but he places his hand over mine.

"Someone is trying to get ahold of you," he says, his voice lazy and hushed.

"Ignore it," I whisper, kissing him again because I don't want this moment to end. It feels too good for me to care, no matter how much they try.

He draws his face back and releases his hold a little. "It must be important. That is the third time it has alerted you."

Oh shit! Aunt Kelly!

I yank out my phone and frantically scroll down. She's sent several new texts. It's hard to concentrate and I have to read them twice before they start making sense. Taking in a deep breath before I have to make any more excuses, I decide to tell Dominic the truth.

"It's my aunt." I pause, watching his expression become more serious. I can tell he's reading my emotions. "She called when I was in my, um, our room. She's worried about Uncle John…" I shake my head. "I mean, her husband. She can't find him. She was devastated and crying—and it's the reason I tried to leave. I said I would help find him." I study his face, expecting him to be pissed, and brace myself for another lecture on how dangerous my actions were, but that doesn't happen. He's not upset at all—in fact, he actually seems almost relieved. I don't have time to analyze it because there's one last message from her I haven't read yet:

> Aunt Kelly: I found him thru his phone.
> Aunt Kelly: He's at the cemetery.
> Aunt Kelly: On my way.

My eyes go wide. She must be talking about this cemetery. I scan the area but there's no sign of him.

"What is it?" Dominic asks, his tone more alert as he pulls up his black hood.

He knows I'm confused—and I am.

Why would Uncle John come here? Is he looking for me? I know he's not here to see Zack; they sure as hell didn't get along. Uncle John doesn't get along with anyone except his gambling buddies.

Dominic reaches for my arm and pulls me to him. "Stay close," he whispers and I follow his gaze.

Uncle John makes his way toward us, looking completely healthy. Someone is by his side. Someone I don't recognize. He's definitely male and enormous, like Dominic, but there's something off about him. Maybe it's the way he walks, with a slightly hunched over back, that's throwing me off?

This can't be good. Dominic is preparing for something. I can feel the anticipation practically radiating from his body.

I need to tell him he can relax.

"It's just my uncle John," I whisper out of the side of my mouth, still watching as they approach. "I'm pretty sure we're safe."

"He is not the one I am concerned about…"

CHAPTER TWENTY-ONE

"WELL, WELL, IF it isn't my little niece," Uncle John singsongs from a few yards away. His demeanor is way off—as if he's gained tons of confidence and a personality.

"Uncle John, what are you doing here?" I ask, genuinely confused.

He cocks his head and smiles sarcastically, like I've just told him a dirty joke. "Why don't you ask your—" He stops and looks up at Dominic and I swear I see his face change. Like he's actually seeing him for the first time and is slightly intimidated. "Friend."

"I don't understand," I admit, craning my neck to look up at Dominic. His eyes flash with a tinge of red directed straight at the big dude standing next to Uncle John.

"Stay away from her, Malum," Dominic bites out.

Holy shit, they know each other?

The bile in his voice sends a chill down my neck and if I didn't know him so well, I would already be running. Instead, I move closer, wrapping both arms tightly around him.

"*Ipsa morietur!*" Malum growls in a deep, sadistic voice, spreading his arms as grotesque, thorn-like wings somehow burst through his flesh. The heavy, sickening smell of copper and sulfur pours down the back of what used to be his arms, sending instant nausea to my gut.

Dear

God...

Dominic shoves me behind him and shouts, "*Esto ab ea!*"

The rage in his voice pierces my eardrums and my hands slam against my ears. I look up only to see his black cloak transform into some sort of metal armor, and then massive, beautiful black wings spread out behind him. They're incredible, even breathtaking, and if I weren't so freaked out right now I'd reach out to touch them.

Dominic stands at least three feet above Malum as they face one another, gearing up to fight. Uncle John runs toward me with an impressive burst of speed, like he was waiting for the chance to pounce. Before I can react, he grabs the collar of my sweater, yanking up and dragging me down the hill. I see Dominic whip his head in my direction but Malum bolts straight for him, forcing him to take his eyes off me and fight.

"Let go of me!" I scream, flailing my arms as I try reaching for a rock embedded solidly in the ground to stop his momentum.

"Shut up! I should have killed you when I had the chance!" Uncle John shouts in a deep voice I barely recognize.

Managing to grasp the rock's edge, I'm able to maneuver my body around, pulling him down with my legs. He lands hard on his back. He may be bigger than me but he's not faster. I have a split second to take control. Images of Papa, who taught me everything I know about getting out of impossible situations, flash in my head. The echo of his voice is still loud and clear: "Stay in control and breathe, Kate..."

Without warning, Uncle John gets to his feet and dives at me with a look of fury I've never seen in his eyes. He misses when I quickly turn, gripping his arm, and we lock eyes. All I see is black, even where the whites should be. I shove my other hand around his shoulder, twisting with all I have. I hear a pop as he drops to his knees and I realize I have a straight shot for his crotch. I draw back my foot but stop when I hear my name.

"Kate! No!" Aunt Kelly screams as she sprints toward us.

Before I know it, Uncle John jerks me up from behind, tightly wrapping his arm around my chest and pushing something sharp against my neck.

"Stay back, Kelly! I swear I'll slit her throat if you take one more step."

Aunt Kelly stops instantly, only feet from us, and I watch her expression change. "John! What...what's wrong with your eyes?" She takes another step.

"Stay away!" he growls, tightening his grip around me as he pushes the knife a little harder into my flesh.

Aunt Kelly's hands go up in surrender and she looks at me with something far more than worry. It's more like devastation. Tears roll down her cheeks and I close my eyes, wishing—no, praying—I can do something, anything to get away from him. But his hold is too tight and if I move even slightly, I have no doubt he'll slit my throat right here. He wants me dead, that much is clear.

Please, Papa...help me...please...

An electric jolt runs through my body and I flinch from the shock. My eyes flash open and somehow I'm free from Uncle John's grip. I watch as Uncle John trips forward in slow motion. We lock eyes as he realizes I got away; he grunts and charges after me, the blade of the knife pointed straight at me.

"John, nooo!" Aunt Kelly shrieks and slams her eyes shut. *"Gladio pereat!"*

113

Whatever she said was in the same language Dominic and Malum used. Maybe Latin? Aunt Kelly knows Latin?

And if I hadn't seen it with my own eyes, I wouldn't have believed it. The knife actually jerks from his hand as if someone yanked it away and goes flying through the air, landing sideways on the ground.

Uncle John's expression changes from fury to confusion. His gaze darts from me to Aunt Kelly, like we've both performed some kind of magic trick. Now he's the docile housedog surrounded by two wild predators. He crouches, ready to fight. A loud thump cracks to the ground and I recognize the spikey, bloody wings. The creature, Malum or whatever he is, doesn't move. He's obviously dead.

My stomach drops because I don't see Dominic anywhere. I want to scream his name or run like hell to find him but I can't because Uncle John pulls up an enormous rock and hurls it straight at me. His strength is frightening and I have to react quickly, ducking the blow. Something pushes me out of the way from behind. I fall to my knees and glance up to see Dominic, back to his hooded self, no wings or armor in sight.

He stops only inches away, his hand going out like he's a priest about to bless his congregation. "*Et abiit post bestiam!*"

Uncle John starts to shake and drops hard to his back. Aunt Kelly sprints toward him but Dominic raises his other hand in warning. The message is clear and she stops, her palms covering her mouth.

"*Et abiit post bestiam!*" Dominic shouts again, only this time, I see Uncle John's eyes change back to normal, no longer solid black

Aunt Kelly gasps so I assume she saw it too.

Uncle John blinks a few times and looks around in a daze. He shakes his head. "Where am I?"

"You are safe," Dominic answers, reaching out to me.

I rush to him and fall into his arms, kissing his neck. I feel something wet on his back and look down at my hand, gasping when I see that it's covered in blood. Dominic stumbles but rights himself as his face goes white. My heart starts pounding in my chest.

I can actually feel his weakness and his willingness to leave his body.

Oh my God, he's bleeding to death!

No!

No!

No!

"Zack!" I scream so loudly my voice cracks.

CHAPTER TWENTY-TWO

DOMINIC STUMBLES AGAIN and I push against him, grunting as I try to steady his enormous frame. Aunt Kelly looks up from tending to Uncle John, who's still in a fog, and rushes to Dominic's other side. Even with both of us holding him he still overpowers our efforts and drops to his knees, his blank face creating a new pit in my stomach.

"We need to get him on his side!" I yell, cringing at the pool of crimson that continues to drain out of him, drenching the knees of my jeans. "Shit, he's bleeding too much!"

"John!" Aunt Kelly shouts. "We need you!"

Her voice, or maybe her urgency, snaps him out of it. He whips his face toward us, quickly scurrying over to help.

"Hurry, press your hand here and push it hard!" I guide Uncle John to the left side of Dominic's back, placing his shaky palm against the deepest gash.

I stand for a second, letting Aunt Kelly and Uncle John help him down. I frantically scan the area for Zack, hoping he heard me.

How can he not know what's going on?!

"Kate," Aunt Kelly screams, "do something!"

What am I supposed to do? The desperation in her voice practically knocks me down as new tears cascade down my cheeks. I collapse next to Dominic's lifeless body. I don't know what to do or how to fix him. His eyes are closed and I can feel him slipping away. My fingers quiver as they gently touch his face—he may have saved my life but he's losing this battle.

"You can't die... You can't die..." I say so softly even I can barely hear my words.

I scoot my body closer and press my lips tenderly to his. He doesn't move or react the way I so desperately want him to, so I close my eyes and kiss him again, willing him to react. It isn't working. It's as if the life has completely drained out of him; it feels like my heart is ripping in half.

Please, Dominic. Please don't leave me...

Without warning, an electric shock bolts through my veins and it's as though I'm being lifted from my body. I'm floating above us, looking down. I see my body next to his, can still feel his lips pressed against mine. I want him to live so badly that in this moment, right here, right now, I will do anything to bring him back—anything. I'm not sure if it's because he already marked me as his mate, but suddenly, it's like I'm releasing all apprehension and bonding myself back to him. I would even give my life for his. Until now, I had no idea how much this man means to me. I—I love him. I am truly, wholeheartedly, with every ounce of my being, in love with this man.

My eyes flash open when Dominic's mouth begins to move. I can feel my energy or my essence or whatever makes me live literally being pulled out of me; I can see it moving from my body into his. Then he inhales so deeply it's like he just took his first breath after being under water for too long. He exhales and I pull back, no longer watching from above as I stare into his eyes, watching them slowly blink back open.

I yank him to me, crying like I've never cried before. It's as if every single bad thing that's happened in my life has finally come to a head. Papa dying, my parents dying, the fire, Zach, Aunt Kelly knowing things she never told me, and now this. I clutch Dominic's neck so tightly, I'm almost surprised when I feel his arms wrap about me. I look up to see those beautiful brown eyes I wanted so desperately to see again.

"Do not cry, my love," he whispers.

At the sound of his voice, I nestle my tear-soaked face further into his chest. His palm cups the back of my head, cradling me safely to him. He's alive, somehow he's alive, and at this point, I don't care how and I don't care why. All that matters is that we're both okay.

I look up at the sound of my name, squinting at the silhouette of a man walking toward us. Dominic's body stiffens, as if ready to lunge, but I squeeze his hand, urging him to wait a second. There's something familiar about him; something in the way he walks—

"Skylar?"

He stops a few feet away. "H-hey Kate," he stutters, looking from me to Dominic, like he's just seen a ghost.

"W-what you doing here?"

He kicks the ground, looking down. "I...uh...I thought I might find you here," he finally says, shoving his hands in his pockets.

"Why?" I don't even try to disguise my confusion.

"I was worried about you." He pauses and looks down again as if embarrassed. "A few days ago, I followed you here and hid behind a headstone." He glances back up. "I watched you run after him into the woods." He nods to Dominic, who rises to his feet, pulling me along with him.

I stay silent and let him keep talking. I know there's more.

"You weren't answering my texts so I decided to try looking for you once more." Skylar stops, shaking his head like he's trying to get his story straight. "When you weren't at the motel, I came here. That's when your uncle and some big dude in a hoodie approached me, asking questions about you." He turns his gaze to Uncle John, who's back to looking clueless as hell.

"Questions—about me?" I ask, slipping both hands around Dominic's arm to keep him close.

Skylar's eyes come back to me. "Yeah. Like if I knew where you were and when I saw you last."

"Did the Demon speak?" Dominic bites out. His question was simple, but I can tell Skylar is frightened of him.

"Demon?" Skylar repeats the word and swallows.

Dominic doesn't answer but a look of realization clouds Skylar's face, as if he just figured out Dominic was referring to the big guy in the hoodie.

"Not that I can remember. He was too busy sniffing the air and giving me dirty looks."

If the situation weren't so serious, that would've made me laugh.

"He knows too much!" Dominic whispers in my ear, his tone riddled with urgency.

I nod and look back to Skylar, realizing his accidental involvement will change his life forever. How the hell am I going to explain the impossible to him? I mean, he's already witnessed the unexplainable, but now he's part of it. Someone I care about, someone who's completely innocent in all this, will have to somehow keep us a secret.

Aunt Kelly, who's been tending to Uncle John, no doubt trying to answer all his questions, cocks her head and walks a little closer. It's obvious she wants to hear what Dominic and I are discussing. Uncle John follows behind.

Dominic glances over to the remains of the Demon, lying on the ground in a sickening, bloody heap of skin guts and bones. "We should go, before the stench of death is detected."

Aunt Kelly's eyes go wide. "We can't just leave him here!" She points her finger at Skylar.

I know what Dominic is thinking before he says a word. "We're not," I answer, with more clarity than I've had in days. "He's coming with us."

.

CHAPTER TWENTY-THREE

A LOOK OF PANIC washes over Skylar's face and he holds up both hands like someone's pointing a gun at him. "Wait! I—I'm not going anywhere!" he screams in a shaky voice.

"You have no choice," I say simply, hoping he doesn't try anything stupid, like trying to get away.

Skylar's gaze shifts from me to Dominic as Aunt Kelly and Uncle John watch from behind us. "I—I won't go. You can't make me!" he shouts, turning around and looking for a way out. He's about to take off but Dominic is way ahead of him, grabbing his collar before he can take even one step.

"You will come. We do not have time for this," Dominic says, his voice calm but fierce.

Skylar stumbles and yanks his body away from Dominic like a little kid who just got in trouble. "I can walk, dammit!"

Dominic steps away, his glare a reminder to behave, and reaches for my hand. "We must go, now!" he says, jerking his head toward the forest.

The gesture doesn't go unnoticed as Aunt Kelly, Uncle John, and Skylar follow us down a slight hill and through the heavily wooded path. It's light enough to see but we have to walk in single file, navigating past thorny vines and low-hang-ing branches. After maybe ten minutes, we finally reach the entrance to the cave.

Dominic stops before going in, looking down at me. "Zack is waiting inside," he says in a low voice.

"Good, I need to talk to him." I try to make my way past him, wondering why he stopped us.

Dominic reaches out, pulling my arm gently back. "Do you think your aunt is ready?" he whispers.

"What do you mean?"

"Zack is not the same as he once was." He glances toward the cave and then back to me. "We need to prepare her."

"She'll be fine," I answer, waving my hand like it's no big deal. "She already knows he's come back."

Dominic shoots me a doubtful look but steps aside for me to lead them in.

The cave is beyond dark, but the torches give off enough light to see the way around. Zack is standing by the huge rock where Dominic's crystals remain lined up. He's wearing a dark cloak with the hood pulled up and for the first time since seeing him again, I notice he gives off a subtle light—almost as if he's glowing. He definitely has an otherworldly look, which is strangely mesmerizing. I freeze for a second, taking it in, when Aunt Kelly comes up to my left.

She's trembling with fear or nerves, I'm not sure which, and squints as she tries to make out who he is. Her eyes go wide and her body wobbles into mine, causing me to stumble. Dominic instantly reacts, catching her by the arms. He shoots me an "I told you" look but I ignore it.

"Zack?" Her voice cracks when she says his name.

He pulls down his hood, revealing his new blue eyes. Aunt Kelly gasps before running into his arms. Zack embraces her warmly, smiling down at her.

"Kate told me it was true...but I...I still can't believe it's really you!" She strokes his face with her palm, studying his features.

Zack leans in, gently kissing her cheek. "Yes, Aunt Kelly, we definitely have some catching up to do, but first..." He stops, looking from me and to Dominic. "First we need to discuss what just happened and what we've now started."

"Wait, what *we* started?" I pop back. "We were attacked!" My words are a little louder than intended, shifting my eyes to Uncle John, who looks slightly in shock as he stares at Zack.

"I'm fully aware of what happened," Zack says calmly. His eyes go to Skylar, who looks confused and scared out of his mind.

"Then where the hell were you when I called for you?" I shout, this time with full intention.

"Clearly, you didn't need me," Zack says, shaking his head. "You will never know your true abilities if you always seek help."

"True abilities?" I scream. "Dominic could have died!"

"Dominic did die," Zack admits, "but you saved him... yourself."

"I kissed him, Zack," I shout, as blood rushes to my face. "I didn't do any saving!" I'm pissed and don't understand why he's being so nonchalant about this.

"He's right," Skylar's shaky voice chimes in. "I saw the whole thing myself. We all did."

Sweet Jesus.

Realization washes over me and my hand goes to my mouth. The floating, the feeling of energy being sucked out of me. Was that me? My power? Did I really bring him back?

"Now do you believe me?" Zack says, smiling. "You've only just begun uncovering your true gifts…"

I knew Zack was right even before the words came out of his mouth. And somehow, I hadn't understood until this very moment. My confidence, or maybe my newfound independence, has tripled over the past couple of days. I can actually feel a change in myself. I'm no longer wallowing; I have a purpose. I don't understand that purpose, but I have a purpose just the same. It's as if the world has become alive, more colorful, and my senses have been magnified.

"Yeah," I say, grinning back at Zack. "I do. I think I do believe you."

"Good, because we still need to talk about the Demon attack," Zack says, looking to Uncle John.

Uncle John perks up, as if suddenly paying attention. "Wait a second, I don't know how the hell you're suddenly alive," his hand waves up and down at Zack, "much less standing in a cave, talking to you about some kind of demon attack, but I swear, I didn't know that guy actually *was* one." His words are defensive, his eyes darting nervously around to each of us.

"That might be true," Zack pauses, "but you *were* taking money from him—right?"

Aunt Kelly's eyes go wide. "Wait, he gave you money? Why?"

I watch Uncle John's Adam's apple rise and fall as he swallows but it seems he's too scared to answer her question.

"You want me to tell her?" Zack asks. "Or would you like to tell us *all* the truth?"

Aunt Kelly's expression shifts to a tight scowl as she straightens up her back like she's preparing herself for more devastating news. Uncle John glances at her and looks down, squeezing his eyes shut as his fingers rub against his forehead.

"I...I needed it to pay someone back," he finally blurts out.

"Dammit, John! Your fucking gambling almost got us all killed!" Aunt Kelly cries, the rage in her eyes sending a chill down my neck. "Do you realize if Kate hadn't been there, Dominic would be dead right now? That *we all* could be dead right now?!"

"That's just it," Zack chimes in. "The Demon," he pauses and looks at me, "was after you, Katie."

"Wait a second, are you saying Uncle John led him to me?" My voice rises an octave. "How could you do that? To pay a debt?!"

"Hold on." Uncle John's hand goes up. "I don't remember anything after meeting that dude in the motel parking lot. I don't even know how I got to the cemetery—I swear."

"The Demon influenced you," Zack explains. "You were under his control by then."

"Well, that explains his black eyes," I say, watching his fear change to confusion.

"We can work out the details later, but for now, we need a plan," Zack says, rubbing his hands together.

"Hold on! The knife." Aunt Kelly interrupts, narrowing her eyes at Uncle John, capturing his full attention. "I did that!" she says like she's just putting the pieces together. "I'm the one who got it away from you!"

"What knife?" Uncle John's eyes dart to each of us as another level of confusion covers his face.

Aunt Kelly takes a deep breath and lets it out slowly. "The one you had around Kate's throat, you son of a bitch!" she shouts, her voice full of fury.

"I swear to God, honey, I didn't know!" Uncle John pleads, but she looks away as if disgusted by the sight of him.

"It doesn't matter now," Aunt Kelly whispers as a single tear drops down her cheek. "When we get home, I'm—" She shakes her head, struggling to speak. "It's over."

Uncle John's face goes white and he rushes to take her hand but she jerks away.

"Please don't, baby. Please don't do this…" His voice drips with anguish and if he were anyone else I might actually feel sorry for him. But I don't. I can't forgive him for treating Aunt Kelly like shit all these years and trying to make up for it with seven little words.

"I hate to break the news," Zack's voice soaks up the dreadful awkwardness, "but no one's going anywhere—at least for now. It isn't safe for any of you and we have to do everything we can to keep you safe."

"Um, that's impossible," Skylar interrupts, frantically looking for an exit. "I—I have football practice! And Thanksgiving is in two days! I can't stay here!"

Zack looks over at Dominic and he nods; apparently they can communicate subliminally. Dominic picks up one of the crystals and hands it to Skylar. "Take this and squeeze it in your hand."

Skylar looks up at Dominic as his fingers fold around the crystal. "What is this?"

"It will help you," Dominic says simply.

Skylar falls silent, squeezing the stone without question, and his knuckles go white. A flash of light completely illuminates the cave; I have to cover my eyes from the blinding light. The cave goes dark after a moment and I cautiously open my eyes, waiting for my vision to adjust back to the darkness. Skylar's gone, nowhere in sight.

"Skylar? Where did you go? Skylar?!" I call for him, realizing how frantic must I sound.

Zack takes my hand. "He's okay. I sent him home. He won't remember a thing."

CHAPTER TWENTY-FOUR

"Y OU SENT HIM home?" I ask, trying to get closer to Dominic, the bright light of the flash still messing with my vision. "Don't they know about him? The Demons, I mean?"

"Unlikely," Zack answers. "I'm pretty sure the only Demon who saw him was Malum and he's dead."

I hear his words but it's still hard to believe Skylar won't remember any of this. "What if he tries to find me again?"

"We'll be ready," Zack replies almost absentmindedly. "Speaking of which...Dominic, there are four crystals remaining?"

He nods, shifting his eyes to me.

Something isn't right.

"Are you going to tell me what's wrong or am I going to have to drag it out of you, like everything else?"

Dominic glances at Zack, then bring his eyes back to me. I can tell he doesn't want to talk about it, but he suddenly blurts out, "I had to earn them."

"Earn them? Why? How?" I ask. His face is a mask of indecision. I wish he'd just elaborate. Why all the secrecy?

"Kate, it does not matter," he says. "I will get more."

Zack sucks in a breath and closes his eyes, shaking his head as if Dominic just shared a secret. A rush of adrenaline mixed with sorrow—or it's maybe dread—begins to churn in my gut. I'm still getting used to the direct line to Dominic's emotions because it's beyond intense. I have to take a step back and reach behind me for a flat surface, anything to keep my knees from buckling. Dominic immediately reacts, catching me before I fall.

"She is weak—maybe I have taken too much from her?" he asks, looking to Zack.

"She only needs rest. Take her to your quarters," Zack says, darting his eyes to Aunt Kelly and Uncle John. "You two, come with me."

Dominic wraps his arms around my back, holding me steady against his chest. I have no choice but to close my eyes. The chaos of the past however long it's been hits me all at once. I hear feet shuffle and low conversation fill up the cave, but my lids are too heavy to keep open. I close them, succumbing to the sudden exhaustion. A pair of hands slip underneath me, lifting me up as if I weigh nothing. I inhale the familiar masculine-with-a-hint-of-rosemary scent of Dominic's skin and sigh. This feels right. It feels like home, which is something I haven't had in a long time. I can finally let go and allow someone else to take care of me.

My body sways back and forth and I manage to force my eyes open for a moment. Darkness surrounds us, but there's a small speck of light at the end of the passageway. The constant motion as the air sears past us makes me wonder. Is he running with me? Are we flying somehow?

Am I dreaming?
Yes, I must be.

LESLIE FEAR

"You are not dreaming, my love," he whispers in my ear. "You are transitioning."

I barely hear his words as everything around me slowly fades to black.

* * *

Heavy footsteps yank me out of a dream, my eyes flashing open and darting around the room. *Where am I?* My mind is fuzzy from what feels like a heavy sleep as I begin to rub my eyes—but wait, I know that walk; I'd know it anywhere. The massive door slowly creaks opens and even before he walks through, I can smell the earth on his warm olive skin. I pull myself up as Dominic's eyes lock with mine and I watch his lips curl into an almost seductive smile.

"Good morning, my love." His deep, hushed voice send goosebumps all over my body and my stomach growls at the smell of bacon and eggs permeating in the air. For a moment, I feel like I have to literally hold myself back from ravaging the tray like a wild animal. I've never been this hungry before. Ever.

"We must discuss a few things," he says, sitting next to me and placing the food tray on my lap. "But first, you should eat."

You don't have to ask me twice.

I force myself to only pick up one strip of what tastes like the most amazing bacon I've ever eaten. I'm not sure if it's because I'm beyond ravenous or if there's something about this place that makes the food taste magical. Dominic tilts his head like he's reading my thoughts and takes my free hand. "From now forward, your senses will be like nothing you have experienced before."

"It's amazing. Did you make this?" I ask between bites.

"No," he answers, looking amused at my enthusiasm. "We have kitchen stewards who make all of our meals."

"You mean like cooks?"

"Yes." The corners of his lips curl up revealing straight, white teeth.

"Very cool. So," I pause, chewing the huge bite of eggs I just shoved in my mouth, "what did you want to talk to me about?"

Dominic looks away for a second and swallows, like he's choosing his words carefully. "Do you feel any differently?" He has something in his hands that I didn't see until now.

"I—I'm not sure. I don't think so, why?"

He shifts, getting closer to me. "While you were sleeping… Well, your body, or I should say your appearance changed slightly."

"What do you mean *changed*?" I accentuate the last word.

"Do not be alarmed." He releases my hand. "It is a natural progression for a Seraph to undergo physical adaptations." He finally reveals what he was holding as he pulls out a mirror and turns it to my face.

I feel my eyes go wide at the reflection staring back. It isn't me, but a complete, one hundred percent enhancement of me. Like I've gone through one of those really cool camera filters with added hair and makeup. My eyes are no longer the chocolate brown they once were. Now, they're what look like a cobalt blue, almost the color of Zack's, but much deeper. And my lashes are thicker and blacker, like they're false, but not. My straight chestnut brown hair is now slightly wavy with cinnamon tones, accentuating my rosy cheekbones and crimson lips. I can still tell it's me, but I look like a different person, or a different version of me. And one thing stands out more than anything else. I actually look older, like I've aged at least five years.

"What—I mean, how did this happen?" I ask as I stare at my reflection.

"The longer you are in a Seraph's presence, the faster the transition happens—it was only a matter of time." Dominic squeezes my hand and pushes away the tray of food, pulling me close.

Ever so gently his lips touch mine. "You are no longer Kate Bassett," he whispers. "You are now officially our Queen."

"I...I don't know what to say." I pull back to look him in the eyes. "I mean, you told me I was Queen but I certainly didn't feel like one. Heck, I'm pretty sure I forced it out of my mind because I didn't really believe it, either." I pause, realizing I'm wearing some kind of a white, silky nightgown. I hold the mirror back up to my face. "But now...now it's all starting to make sense. The bond we share and the fact that I could actually breathe life back into you..."

"That is your biggest gift." The expression on his face becomes more serious, his voice more stern. "But you need to use it wisely. You must be certain the person you save is worthy of being saved."

"Worthy?" I repeat.

"Yes. Otherwise the process will take too much out of you."

"Okay, so, I take a nap or something and recharge?"

"It doesn't work that way." Dominic's nostrils flare a little and he takes the mirror from my hand. "Saving someone unworthy could kill you."

Gulp.

"So as long as I don't try to save a Demon or someone evil, I'll be fine?"

The apprehension draping his face is starting to make me nervous but I keep going.

"I mean, now that I can sense things and I know you'll always be close, it shouldn't be rocket science," I rattle off, trying to make it sound a little less ominous in my head. "To know if someone is worthy, I mean. Right?"

"Partly true, yes." His expression doesn't waver. "However, like yesterday, I was not able to be at your side."

He's right. Aunt Kelly and I were on our own. But we did manage to fight off the Demon who had taken over Uncle John.

"Thankfully, Malum is dead," Dominic points out. "He is, or I should say, *was* one of the most powerful Demons in the underworld. But there will be more and we must be prepared." He places the mirror next to the bed and takes my other hand.

"Like getting more crystals?" I ask.

"Let me worry about those," he says in a hurry, and it's obvious that topic is off limits.

"Well," I take a deep breath, "I guess I should brush up on my fighting skills and learn some Latin." I smile, trying to lighten the mood.

"That will all come to you naturally. Soon, you will discover more physical abilities and you will also begin to easily interpret different languages."

Wait, he's right. I did manage to free myself from Uncle John's grip. And apparently the Latin will come on its own. I wonder what else I can do…

As if reading my mind, Dominic grins and nods. "Yes, you can also teleport."

"I thought it was Aunt Kelly who helped me escape, but it was me…I did that?" I whisper, trying to replay it in my head. "Hold on, the knife," I blurt out. "She yelled something in Latin and it practically ripped its way out of Uncle John's hand! That really was her."

"Yes, as we discussed before, her gift, among many others is telekinesis," he explains as my mind begins to race with more questions.

"Will she transform?"

"Yes, but not as significantly as you."

"When? Will her eyes change?"

"They already have. They are no longer brown, they are green."

Holy crap.

"Okay, but I don't understand how she already knew Latin," I say, my eyes suddenly dropping down to his sexy, plump lips.

He must sense I'm slightly turned on; he smiles and scoots a little closer. The crazy-enhanced scent of his skin is starting to arouse me in a whole new way and I have to practically talk myself out of ripping off his cloak.

His eyelids grow heavy and I know he's feeling it too. He wraps his arms around me, pulling me close enough to kiss but answers my question first, his voice low and deep. "Her transformation had already started before the attack. It is typically gradual, except for Seraph Masters. And you, of course."

I nod and look into his eyes but don't say a word. I want him to kiss me. I want to feel his body against mine. I want him like a woman wants a man. Slowly, he leans in, tenderly touching his lips to mine as his palm gently cups the back of my head. He presses a little harder, opening his mouth, the rush of his warm breath sending another surge between my legs. It's glorious and stimulating and I don't want it to stop. His hands begin to move to my torso, rubbing my back as his delicious tongue dances with mine.

I want more.

I need more.

Suddenly he pulls back and takes in a deep breath, like he's coming up for air. "We cannot let this go too far," he whispers. "We have not been officially joined."

Pushing back the heavy blanket of lust, I try to process his words. "You mean like," I pause to wrap my brain around it, "get married?" I swallow, our faces only inches apart.

"If you will have me, yes."

CHAPTER TWENTY-FIVE

THUNDEROUS POUNDING ERUPTS without warning, shattering my thoughts, and I snap my head toward the beating. Dominic immediately goes into warrior mode, rushing his enormous frame to the door without making a sound. His cloak practically comes to life on its own, wrapping its way around him as tiny metal looking spikes begin poking up through the fabric. Another set of deafening strikes hammer against the door; I have no doubt that someone is trying to beat it down by hand.

Dominic glances back at me with caution in his eyes, advising me to stay silent, and yanks up on the latch, pulling the massive door open and protectively angling himself in front.

"I thought I smelled you in here." Uncle John somehow twists past Dominic, pushing towards me. His eyes are completely black, his voice not his. He leaps over Dominic as if he suddenly has super powers and lands next to me.

I scramble to get to my knees. I can almost see the Demon inside of him, contorting his features like an animal.

"Now you will die!" he snarls, holding something shiny in his hand as he thrusts back his arm. The black rage in his glare feels like pure evil pulsating directly at me.

Before Dominic can get to me, Uncle John lunges, the blade of his knife catching the torchlight. I'm faster and block him with my arm. He loses his balance and Dominic is on him, wrapping his massive arms around his shoulders and stopping him from falling. He effortlessly grabs Uncle John's weapon hand and rips it off with a sickening tearing sound. Blood splatters everywhere and the beast inside him roars in agony.

The room floods with huge, cloaked warriors. They surround my bed, protecting me as they lift Uncle John from Dominic's hold, his body thrashing around.

"Keep the Demon inside him. I need the beast to talk," Dominic orders, picking up the bloody hand and thrusting it angrily at Uncle John. Another warrior reaches out, catching the dripping stump before it hits the wall as they take him away.

Dominic's back is to me, facing the door as it slams shut, his shoulders rising and falling, trying to catch his breath. But it's not breathing he's trying to get under control. It's pure rage. And I can feel it.

The animalistic cries of the Demon echo down the hallway and he turns to me with a warning expression. "I may have to kill him."

All I can do is nod because I'm still replaying the sickening sight of Uncle John's hand being ripped from his arm. And all the blood. There was so much blood.

"I will not be long." Dominic leans down and practically smacks my forehead, with his lips, snapping off the horrific images in my head. "Do not leave this room, Kate," he reminds me, his voice firm and more controlled.

"Wait!" I interrupt. "I'm coming with you!" I fly off the bed, scanning the room for something other than this long, white nightgown.

"No!" Dominic bites out, startling me out of my frantic search. "It is too dangerous."

"Too dangerous?" I allow my sarcasm to flood out. "I think we both just proved we can take him."

He cocks his head, acknowledging my bravery. "I am sorry, but I cannot allow it. You are not ready."

"Oh, I'm ready," I feel my nose flare. "That asshole just tried to kill me! Again!"

"You do not understand!" Dominic shouts. "Demons will stop at nothing to manipulate." He shakes his head like he's pushing away a memory. I can tell he's experienced it firsthand. "They will taunt you. Reveal things about you that they cannot possibly know."

Blood rushes to my face. I'm not sure if it's because I've just been attacked or I'm starting to get pissed. I'm pretty sure it's a combination of both.

"I'm going." I push an arm through the extremely expensive-feeling red velvet robe I found hanging in the armoire.

Dominic's breath catches and I look up. He crosses one leg behind him, bending at the waist as he lowers his head. He's in a full bow, like I've never seen before, and for a millisecond, I'm thrust back into the awareness of my position here. I don't need to ask permission. I have leverage. I have a trump card.

"You may be my Watchman, but last time I checked, I am your Queen," I say, squaring my shoulders.

He looks up as if surprised, his powerful eyes locking with mine. He knows he can't say no despite the danger and despite my stubbornness. The expression on his face is pure resentment but I ignore it, trying to hide the fact that I can feel it, too.

Fastening the last button, I walk toward him, gathering up my now wavy, auburn hair from underneath the high, stiff collar. I stop at the door and glance up at him, hoping the discontent in his eyes is no longer there. But he's not going to give in, he's livid. And now I've just belittled the man I love.

Closing my eyes, I pull in a deep breath, managing to keep my head up as I try to disguise my regret. I take a step past him, reaching for the latch, but Dominic's hand pushes it away and he opens the door. I don't dare look up, the daggers in my gut are already too sharp. I can fix this, I know I can—but until then, Uncle John's day is about to get a whole lot worse.

I wait in the hallway for him to walk past me. "C'mon," I say, "let's have a chat with the son of a bitch."

Dominic's cloak swishes around his athletic body like a second skin as he starts down the long hallway, never once looking down at me. I have to rush to keep up with him; I wish I could apologize with just a look. Anything to make him understand I didn't mean to upset him. But the opportunity is missed and I follow closely behind. I have no clue where we're going and I'm half wondering if he'll lead me to the wrong room just to spite me. The anger I felt radiating from him has now changed to dread, confirming what I fought so hard for. He's not taking me to the wrong room, he's definitely taking me to Uncle John and now I'm starting to get scared. What have I done? I've seen the Demon up close. Maybe Dominic's right. Maybe I'm not ready for this.

The long, torch-lit hallway is eerily quiet, emphasizing Dominic's gut-wrenching silence. Our footsteps echo harshly off the stone floors. I know I can't do this without his help. We can't face Uncle John without a united front. I have to fix this. I reach out to take his hand but stop just before our fingers touch. I can feel he's not ready; he's still too upset with me. My mind races as I rehearse my apology over and over again, tears blurring my vision. I wipe away the wetness, trying to hide any trace of them. I have to stay strong. I know I can't look weak—especially to Uncle John.

Dominic glances down. He knows I'm shaken but a second later jerks his head forward. We stop just feet away from a floor-to-ceiling iron gate. It's ancient, that much I'm sure of, and I watch in disbelief as he waves his hand in front, the latch somehow unlocking and the gate swinging open. We're several steps in when the sound of metal sliding on groaning gears makes me look back to see the gate glide into its original position and lock into place.

I'm farther away from Dominic than I want, so I catch up. The longer we walk the darker it gets. It's as if we're heading lower and lower underground. I can definitely feel the tension emitting from him. There's a metal door just to our right. He pauses and takes in a deep breath, closing his eyes. I have no doubt that behind the layers of thick steel, my Uncle John is in there—waiting.

Dominic opens his eyes and looks down at me, his expression practically dripping with caution. "You must not allow him to anger you. It is what he wants."

I nod, swallowing back the bile creeping its way to my throat, the all too familiar sharp needles hungrily pricking away at my flesh. It's game time and we both know it. My hands start to shake but this time he reaches for them, pulling me close. His enormous arms hold me tightly and he kisses the top of my head. I pull back and look up, finally seeing the warm, forgiving gaze I begged for only minutes ago. His forehead meets mine and he shivers, perhaps feeling how frightened I am. He pulls me into another hug and whispers, "*Te amo.*"

I don't need a translation for his beautiful words; I know exactly what they mean. I nuzzle against his chest, his amazing scent a relief. I try like hell to push back the new tears threatening to make their way down my cheeks and look back up into his beautiful eyes.

"I love you, too."

CHAPTER TWENTY-SIX

Dominic's lips curl up slightly, sending a warm sensation through my body. If we weren't about to have a conversation with a nasty Demon, I'd be all over him. Dominic's expression changes and he squares his shoulders, like he's suddenly reprograming his thoughts.

He pulls back, taking both of my hands and gently squeezes. "Remember what I said." He narrows his eyes, his face stony. "He is not your Uncle John, Kate. There is no good in him. Do not allow him to manipulate your feelings."

I nod, gazing up at his handsome, chiseled face. He smiles and my confidence is boosted as I take in a cleansing breath. I have no doubt Uncle John's possession is killing Aunt Kelly but I can't worry about her now. He tried to kill me and I'm positive he won't stop until he succeeds. I smile, trying to hide my apprehension. I know whatever awaits us behind that steel door, we will face it together. "Let's kick some ass," I say with more confidence than I feel.

Dominic smiles again but this time it's drenched with caution. He knows I'm nervous as hell—my hands are already trembling. "The Demon is restrained and cannot physically harm you," he says. "And remember what I said. You must be strong. You must control your emotions."

I nod, stepping past him into a room that resembles a huge metal box. There are no windows and no stone, only metal. I'm surprised to see dim halogen lights attached to wire conduit high above me. It's the first time I've seen electricity anywhere. I zero in on a chair placed directly in the center of the room— the same chair Uncle John is sitting in—reminding me of those police interrogation rooms I've seen on TV. His arms are tied behind his back, his eyes closed, chin to his chest. His legs are bound together and blood is pooling on the floor around him, no doubt from Dominic ripping off his hand. Other than that, he looks unharmed.

I take a few quiet steps, not really wanting to engage, when he slowly raises his head, his solid black eyes locking in on mine. And then he smiles. It's not an ordinary smile, though. It's frightening and drenched in evil sophistication. Goose-bumps cover my flesh and if I could turn around and take off in a dead run, I would because clearly, the Demon is still alive and well inside him.

"Well, well, if it isn't my pretty little niece, the new Queen," he says in a low growl, seductively looking me up and down. "I'd bow," he struggles a bit to accentuate his point, "but as you can see, I'm a little tied up." The slight humor in his tone is overpowered by the sound of at least three other voices.

The prickly needles in my gut quickly turn to nausea as the foul odor of death fills the room. Dominic wasn't kidding; this is for real, this is game on. I can't believe that just one single human being can possess what seems like a world of evil. I have to keep calm. I have to stand up to him, no matter how scared I am right now.

LESLIE FEAR

"Uncle John," I acknowledge him, trying to sound more confident than I feel, keeping myself as close to Dominic as I can. I'm so not ready for this but it's too late. I've made my bed and know I have to keep it together. I can't show any fear.

"Come for a little chat?" the voices coming from his mouth ask in unison, sounding like three different personalities are speaking at once.

"Yes," I say honestly. "Who are you?"

Laughter erupts, as if I've told him a funny joke. I take a step closer and Dominic mirrors my actions, staying close by my side. Uncle John notices and stops laughing, his black eyes practically glaring through me.

"Ahh, why not come closer to me?" He puckers his lips. "Give your uncle John a little kiss. It'll be just like old times." Another wave of nausea churns my stomach when I think back to the many times he tried to molest me.

"You are disgusting," I bite out, fury beginning to rage through my veins.

He looks surprised. "What, you didn't enjoy our little bedroom talks?" He cocks his head and gives me a creepy, leering smile. "I thought they were, hmm, how should I put it? Entertaining." The evil sarcasm in his tone makes me want to puke as my anger begins to boil, overriding how scared I was only seconds ago

"Watch it," I say, trying to stay calm. "Or I'll have Dominic rip off your other hand."

Uncle John's eyes go wide and he takes in a dramatic breath, like he's scared to death. "Ah, how adorable that you think I actually give a shit *what* you do to this body." He laughs. "I mean, let's face it, your uncle John probably deserves it, don't you think? All those late nights he came into your room, staggering from too many cheap beers." He chuckles, obviously en-

144

joying himself. "Seriously, I don't know how you managed to stop him every single time." He pauses, narrowing his eyes as if he's calculating how much I can take. "It's a good thing you did. It would have been quite the scandal if he'd gotten you pregnant but couldn't knock up his own wife."

"You son of a bitch!" I scream, scrambling toward him as I throw my arm back to punch his face.

Dominic reacts, his arms wrapping securely around me, holding me back like I'm some kind of attack dog. "You must control your anger," he whispers in my ear but I barely hear him over my own heavy breathing.

I yank myself from his grip and look back to Uncle John, who looks thoroughly entertained.

"What? Too much?" He grins, bursting into laughter.

If I could kill Uncle John with my bare hands right now, I'd do it. Dominic tried to warn me, even tried to tell me I wasn't ready—but I didn't want to listen. I thought I could handle it. And here I stand, totally prepared to murder my aunt's husband. Or at least the demon inside him. Killing the bastard would be a bonus.

Dominic leans close to my ear and whispers, "I can finish this."

Of course he knows I'm questioning what the hell I've done. But none of it matters now and I look up into his reddish-brown eyes, nodding my decision to keep going. I have to see this through even if I have to learn the hard way. It's how I've learned everything else in my life, why stop now?

"I'm okay," I whisper back, trying to calm myself as I catch him shake his head. I know he wants to handle this and would rather I not be here, but I can't leave. I need answers for Aunt Kelly, hell, even for myself if nothing else. How long has he been manipulated by the Demon? What kind of damage has been done?

Dominic releases me and I turn to Uncle John, resisting the urge to slap the condescending smirk off his face. This time I pretend he's someone else, not the uncle I'm unfortunately related to.

"Who are you and why are you doing this to him?" I keep my voice as calm as possible.

The Demon lowers his head just a tad but keeps his eyes on me. "Good old Uncle John and I have been acquainted for quite some time now."

"Okay," I clip back, "but why?"

"You know why, Queen Kate."

"No, I don't," I reply, trying to keep my cool. "Why don't you enlighten me?"

The Demon closes his eyes and rolls his head around on his neck. "He needed our help."

"Stop jacking around and tell me."

The Demon laughs. "Why don't you ask him?" he dares. "He's here, you know. Watching us. Listening to everything we're saying."

"Let him go first!" I say, raising my voice louder than intended. I've never liked Uncle John, I hate him for everything he's tried to do to me and has done to my aunt, but I can't stomach her reaction if anything else happens to him. Especially if I have something to do with it or could possibly prevent it.

"Nah, I like it here. But don't you worry your pretty little head." He smiles, mocking me with his words. "He's not gonna last much longer with me around…"

CHAPTER TWENTY-SEVEN

THE DEMON'S WORDS are like a punch in the gut and suddenly, I want more than just answers. I want to save Uncle John's life. Not for me but for Aunt Kelly. I can't allow this monster to destroy him, no matter how horrible he's been to me.

Dominic leans down and whispers, "You must demand the Demon to reveal himself. You have more power over him and he knows it. Get his name and it will weaken his hold. Separate him from his host." He pauses and takes my hand. "But be quick, we do not have much time."

I nod and glance back up into the Demon's black eyes. He's still smiling back at me but I can tell he's in pain as fresh blood pools behind him, dripping from his bandaged wrist.

"Tell me your name," I demand in a low, authoritative tone, keeping my gaze glued to his.

Laughter erupts again from the Demon's mouth but I try to ignore it. "Why are you so protective of him?" he asks, and I can tell he's trying to avoid the question. "It's not like he's ever done you any favors. Well, none that you've allowed." He shifts in his chair and winks, his smile widening. "If you know what I mean."

"Tell me your name, Demon!" I raise my voice even more, not holding back, and his expression suddenly becomes serious. I'm not sure what changed but I feel compelled to keep going. "Tell me!" I scream. "Now!"

The Demon begins to shake violently, as if I've unleashed a pack of wolves inside him. I take a step to my right to get closer to Dominic, watching the Demon in Uncle John's body contort grotesquely, bucking against the restraints. Without warning, the chair begins to lift from the floor, levitating slightly as deep growls begin filling the room from all directions. Dominic pulls his cloak around me, raising his hand and pointing.

"*Quis es?!*" he roars, his voice reverberating off the walls and overpowering the Demon's growls. The chair slams to the floor, making Uncle John's head wobble like an infant. I cover my mouth with my hands, stifling a scream. I can't tell if he's asleep or...

Shit!

I scramble to get to him but Dominic pulls me back. He glares down at me, the warning in his eyes is palpable. "Stay here!" he demands, advancing on the Demon.

I can't see the Demon's face. His head hangs lopsided off his neck and from where I'm standing it doesn't look like he's breathing. Dominic gets close enough to reach out and push on his shoulder but the Demon doesn't move.

Dominic glances back at me, making sure I haven't moved, I'm sure, then shifts his feet, kicking the side of the Demon's shoe. The movement must have awakened him, or he was totally faking it, and he slowly raises his head.

His smile is slow and cruel, like he's having a blast screwing with us. "You want my name?" he asks, his voice like gravel as he looks straight at me. "Not before a little kiss from the Queen."

Without warning, the door flies open, pounding against the wall before it slams shut, echoing in the room for another deafening couple of seconds.

The Demon shuffles in his chair, pulling himself up like he's preparing himself for battle. "Well, well, well, if it isn't the Master himself." He chuckles. "Looks like someone called in the big guns."

Zack walks methodically into the room, glaring at the Demon, the loud clicking from his shoes driving the point home that he means business. I'm beyond relieved that he's here. The Demon's expression is filled with mockery, but there's something else behind it. Could it be fear? Apprehension?

"Come to help your little sissy and her boyfriend, I see," the Demon spouts off. "I mean, her husband-to-be." He directs his eyes to me and then to Dominic. "Oh and you better be careful, you two," he singsongs, "I don't think a pregnant Queen wearing white on her wedding day sends a very good message."

Before I even look at Dominic, I can feel the lava bubbling through his veins. The Demon is trying to piss him off and he's doing an excellent job. Clearly a strategic move. I'm pretty sure the Demon thinks that if he can somehow keep the attention on everyone else but him, maybe he'll have a fighting chance.

Zack stops just next to Dominic and me but keeps his eyes locked on the Demon's black eyes. "That's enough!" he bites out. "Tell us your name!"

The Demon laughs again like this is all child's play. "Tsk, tsk, Master Zack," he mocks then coughs a little, and I can see his skin going whiter by the second. "You're seriously going to have to do better than that."

Zack leans over to Dominic and whispers, "She shouldn't be here. She's not ready." He glances at me, thinking I didn't hear him.

149

Dominic stays silent, ignoring Zack, and looks back at the Demon, who continues to suck the life out of Uncle John. "You will tell me your name, Demon," he commands, pulling a cross out of his cloak.

It's not just an ordinary cross, it's a freaking masterpiece that looks like it could be from the Middle Ages. It's at least fifteen inches long and the surface is beautifully carved in brilliant gold with ruby red stones set on each end. They're the most spectacular sparkling red I've ever seen. If I didn't know any better I'd swear it was yanked straight off of King Arthur's tomb or at least the Smithsonian.

"Tell. Me. Your. Name!" Dominic pauses between each word, and this time, it's as if each letter is being laser cut into the Demon. Screams and horrific, animalistic cries shoot out of his mouth. A rush of sadness, anger, and resentment pours into me. I nearly fall to the ground but Dominic pulls me up, wrapping his cloak around my body.

"I am Zull!" The Demon's words sound like they're being ripped from of his mouth one single syllable at a time.

Zack grabs the cross from Dominic's hand and moves closer. The Demon twists back and forth, contorting his body like he's fighting his way out of a straightjacket and Zack takes advantage of the moment and touches the thick cross to Uncle John's forehead. A horrendous sizzle echoes through the room, and his skin smokes, branded by the cross.

"Go back to hell where you belong!" Zack commands, shaking something at him from a small white bottle.

Otherworldly shrieks and screams from voices I haven't heard yet blast around the room and I slam my eyes shut, tightening my grip around Dominic's waist.

"I command you, Zull! Leave this body!" my brother shouts. "Leave this body now!"

On Zack's last word the room goes completely quiet. The quiet is so complete it's deafening on its own. What happened? Did we actually get rid of the Demon? Could it even be a possibility? It's hard to believe since he fooled us once already.

I open my eyes when I hear the sound of shuffling feet, lifting my head to look out from underneath Dominic's cloak. Zull, or Uncle John, or whoever the hell he is, is still in the chair but this time it's pretty clear: he's gone. Or at least he sure looks that way. Zack crouches behind him and I watch as Uncle John's arms are freed, swinging to his sides—one clearly missing a hand. But he's too white. It looks as though every ounce of life has been completely drained out of him.

"Hurry!" my brother calls. "We need to get him to the infirmary!"

Before Dominic can ask, I give him a quick nod to let him know I'm okay before he abruptly lets go and rushes to help Zack. I follow, hoping I can do something, anything other than completely freaking out when Dominic swoops my uncle up like he weighs nothing. He glances at Zack and then to me and shakes his head. I don't want to believe it. I can't believe it. It can't be too late.

"No!" I scream. "Do something!"

Without hesitation, they both rush toward the door, sprinting down the dim corridor as I try several times but fail to see Uncle John's face. He's no longer bleeding but the bandages around his wrist, once completely white, are drenched in blood. His body looks artificial, almost like a rag doll, moving awkwardly with each thump of Dominic's rushed stride.

It feels as though we've been running uphill, around corners, and along stretches of long hallways for miles until finally, Zack slows down and stops outside a set of huge metal double doors. He shoves one side open for us to pass and I watch in awe as a team of three men and two women surround Dominic. They take Uncle John's body and place him on an operating table.

"I'm not getting a pulse!" one of the men shouts.

"Martha!" another man yells over his shoulder. "I need three units of O neg, stat!"

"Yes, doctor," she says, handing him a crimson bag as the other woman begins CPR.

I watch in horror as they go to work, hoping like hell they can bring him back. Dominic takes my hand and I look up. He tilts his head toward the door and I follow his lead into the hallway.

"We must tell your Aunt," he says, glancing past me at the sound of someone approaching. Hurried footsteps, too close together to be male, become louder the closer they get and I have to squint before I realize Aunt Kelly is running straight for us.

"Where is he?" she screams, completely out of breath.

My eyes go to the double doors and Aunt Kelly wastes no time taking off in a run, but Dominic reaches out and pulls her back.

"Let go of me!" she screams, trying to yank her arm from his grip.

"Wait!" I say, knowing exactly why Dominic stopped her. He releases her and immediately moves in front of the double doors.

"Aunt Kelly, he's—he's not..."

"Get out of my way!" she screams at Dominic, not even listening to me.

I yank her other arm so hard I almost apologize. She jerks her eyes in my direction—eyes that used to be a dark brown but are now a new shade of deep green—and my breath hitches.

"You have to stop!" I shout, struggling to keep her from getting away. "Aunt Kelly, please! He's dead!"

She drops to her knees. Zack rushes to her side as her palms cover her face but her cries are loud and clear. Guilt slams into me. I kneel down to touch her shoulder but she flinches, pushing my hand away, like she already knows it's my fault.

And she's right. It is.

All of it is...

CHAPTER TWENTY-EIGHT

M Y HAND GOES to Aunt Kelly's shoulder again. "I'm so sorry," I murmur, over and over again. I slowly kneel down to her side and she lets me console her, my fingers gently stroking her hair. I'll do anything to help take away her pain.

She raises her head as tears stream down her cheeks. "Why, Kate?" she asks, her voice barely a whisper. "Why does everyone have to die around you?" Her new green eyes stay locked with mine, her words piercing my heart, each letter chiseling away a chunk at a time. I can't take it. I can't take seeing her this way. She's right; I must be cursed. Everyone I'm close to really has died, one way or the other. I can't allow this to happen—I have to make this right or at least try.

"Please don't cry." I try to swallow the new lump in my throat, darting my eyes to Zack and then back to her. "I know what to do."

Aunt Kelly's brows push together as confusion blankets her face. I smile, kissing the side of her face and rising to my feet. "Be right back."

Dominic doesn't move aside as I approach the double doors. He remains standing guard and I watch his expression change.

"Don't do it, Kate," he warns, his voice so low it's almost a whisper.

"Dominic, you need to step aside," I order, staring at him with as much intensity as I can muster.

"It is not right," he shakes his head, "and you know it."

I glance back at Aunt Kelly, wondering if I'm making a huge mistake. She meets my gaze, wiping away fresh tears with the sleeve of her shirt.

I have no choice.

"Please don't make this difficult," I plead but he doesn't budge.

Frustration floods my initial reluctance and I realize I'm going to have to use a different tactic—something instinctual that might appeal to his duty towards me.

Keeping my eyes glued to his, I clear my throat. "Seraph Warrior, I command that you allow me to pass!"

A look of resentment washes over Dominic's face, or maybe he's simply pissed. But I'm pretty sure he can't deny my request. *Not his Queen.*

He pulls his eyes away from mine and bows his head slightly. I know it's killing him to obey me as his hand slowly pushes the door. I step past him, trying not to think about what just happened. I see the doctors and nurses still attempting to bring life back to Uncle John's lifeless body.

I approach the doctor in charge, tapping his shoulder just before he stops counting his chest compressions. His eyes go wide when he glances up at me, confused. His forehead glistens with sweat as I place my hand on Uncle John's cool arm.

"It's okay, you did your best," I assure him. "Can you please give us a minute?"

I can see Zack and Dominic standing side by side just inside the doors, watching everything. Watching me. Zack nods

155

his permission for them to leave and one by one the team stops what they're doing and files out of the room.

I look down at Uncle John's body, gently touching his cool face before glancing over at my brother and my husband-to-be. Their disapproving expressions make what I'm about to do even harder.

I have to do it. Aunt Kelly simply can't go through another death. Not when I can do something about it.

I lean down over his face, never imagining that I would place my lips anywhere near his, but I press down anyway. Nothing happens at first and I open my eyes, watching for a reaction, hoping it's not too late. After a moment, his body jerks like he's been shocked. Startled, I pull back, but the connection has been made and I'm immediately sucked back down to him as he takes in a deep breath. His hand presses my body even closer to his and I'm suffocating, my arms flailing as I struggle to get free. A sharp sting sears down my throat, sending crippling pain throughout my body. Fear traps my thoughts and I try again to tear myself away before someone grabs me from behind, breaking Uncle John's hold.

I collapse in Dominic's arms, finally able to take a breath as I clutch my chest from the lingering pain. Zack stands over Uncle John, who's already sitting up and looking around, confused as hell.

"W—where am I?" he asks, darting his no-longer-black eyes around the room.

Before Zack can reply, Aunt Kelly comes flying in the room. "John!" she screams, wrapping her arms around him as she nearly pushes him down. "You're alive!" Her voice is full of relief and joy as she kisses his lips, his face, his cheek. "You're alive..."

I watch the awkward reunion, Dominic's arms still wrapped around my waist. The pain in my chest is starting to go away but my eyelids feel like they have weights attached to them. I can barely keep my body upright but before I can ask for help, Dominic scoops up my legs, cradling me as he walks out the infirmary double doors. His steady stride is familiar and comforting, making it easy to give in to the exhaustion.

"Dominic," my brother calls out to him and he turns around, "she needs rest, but stay with her." He pauses. "I'll come by in the morning to check on her."

Dominic nods but doesn't say a word. My body aches all over, like I have the flu, and I can no longer keep my eyes open. I snuggle closer to him, reveling in the safety of his incredible scent, but his arms keep me just far enough away to reveal he's not happy with me. Not even a little bit.

I'm too exhausted to care. His steps echo a steady rhythm off the stone walls and everything starts to drift away…

I'm awoken by hushed whispering across the room. I have to really focus on the blurry figures standing just feet away. The voices help. It's Dominic, in his usual long, black cloak, and Zack in a white button down with the sleeves rolled up and black slacks.

"She's awake," Zack whispers, walking toward me as Dominic follows behind.

I smile but their expressions are way too serious to notice. *Uh, oh. Now what?*

"How are you feeling?" Zack asks, and now his scowl is starting to make me nervous.

"I…I'm fine." I pull myself up but my head slams back down to the pillow, throbbing from the quick motion.

"You're not fine," Zack deadpans. "And you have no idea what you've done."

"What are you talking about?" I rub my temples, hoping to press some of the pain away.

Zack turns to look at Dominic, then back to me. "You shouldn't have done it, Katie." He spoke in barely a whisper, but I can still hear his words loud and clear.

"What?" I say, pushing the covers back in an attempt to show my frustration. "Saved my uncle's life?"

"Yes!" he shouts, looking around the room bashfully, as if he didn't mean to raise his voice.

Fighting the urge to keep my head on the pillow, I pull myself up again. Nausea hits my gut and threatens its way up my throat. I take in a breath to refocus, trying to hold back my frustration while also attempting not to hurl all over myself as my eyes shift back and forth between them. "Let me give you a little reminder." I pause, swallowing the acidy bile trying to make its way to my mouth. "Nobody handed me a freaking guidebook on how to become an entirely different person in such a short amount of time." I cough as my anger continues to build. "Much less become a Goddamned Queen! So I suggest you chill on judging my every move!"

"Watch your language!" Zack shouts, completely ignoring my rant.

"Seriously?" I yell back. "It's like I can't do anything right! I clearly don't know what I'm doing! Hell, I'm not even sure I want it to begin with!"

Zack's brows push together like the answer is obvious. "You don't have a ch—"

"Yeah, yeah," I interrupt. "It's my destiny, my duty and all that shit. Well, you can fire me and find someone else! I only did what I thought was right!"

"That's just it," Zack says, his new blue eyes blazing even bluer. "Everything you do, every single decision you make is completely up to you." He stops and shakes his head. "We have no say so once your mind is made up."

I have to swallow again to push back another wave of nausea.

Holy shit.

"Then why is everyone so upset? Like I said, I only did what I thought was right. Hell, I didn't even do it for me, I did it for Aunt Kelly."

"We know..." Dominic chimes in, his deep tone redirecting my thoughts.

"Then how can you be so pissed? How can it be a bad thing?" I plead, looking back and forth between them. "I saved him for her."

"Because, Katie," Zack says, his voice soft and low, as if attempting to dial back our high emotions, "you brought back a Demon."

"Wait a second, what? The Demon was gone!" I pause, waiting for them to agree. "You both saw him leave. We all did."

"Yes," Zack answers. "Technically. But the risk outweighed the act. You could have died." He looks down, as if it hurts just thinking about it. "Only time will tell if it was the right thing to do. And for the next couple of days, you're going to feel like you've been hit by a Mack truck."

CHAPTER TWENTY-NINE

Zack reaches for my hand with a concerned smile that barely reaches his eyes. "Get some rest," he reminds me, leaning down to kiss my forehead. He whispers something in Dominic's ear, but this time I can't hear his words. "We'll talk about this later," he says, holding the door open for Dominic.

"Dominic, wait," I say, stopping him from going any further. "Please talk to me."

His back is to me so I can't see his face, but I hear the door close. My heart feels like it's in my throat. He doesn't want to stay—I can practically smell it on him.

"You must rest," he whispers, but there's something else behind his tone. Something I can't quite put my finger on. Could it be sorrow? Disappointment? I'm not sure, but it feels a little like both.

"Please don't leave." My voice cracks on the last word and I silently pray he gives in.

I feel like throwing up when his head drops but this time, it's not from possibly resurrecting a Demon. He doesn't want to talk. Hell, I'm pretty sure he doesn't even want to be in the same room with me.

"I'm…I'm sorry," I get out so quickly I'm not exactly sure which part I'm sorry about—saving Uncle John or pulling rank on him. *Again.* Either way, I can't blame him. I put his life, my brother's life, and even my own life in danger. It's obvious I'm not cut out to make serious life decisions, no matter how much I've physically changed. I can't be a ruler.

A flood of tears spills down my cheeks and I pull the sheet up to cover my eyes. A sudden hand on my back keeps me from breaking down. I look up to see Dominic gazing down at me with an expression I've never seen before. It looks a lot like forgiveness. I hope I'm right because if this is something else, like pity, I really am going to puke.

"There are things you must understand, Kate," he says, taking a seat next to me and cupping my face in his palm.

"I know." My voice is only a whisper as I lick another salty tear that somehow escaped.

He moves a little closer. "If I am to be your mate," his fingers wrap around mine and we lock eyes, "I will be your equal—and nothing less."

I know why he's saying this. And I deserve every word.

"I agree." I reach for his other hand. "I never meant to hurt you. Truly."

He grins, and my heart soars. The relief on my face must show or he simply feels it because his smile deepens. "I know," he says, accepting my apology. His face falls and he looks away as his brows push together. "I came very close to losing you, Kate. I do not ever—" He stops and swallows, the words too painful to say aloud. "You have so much to learn, but you *must* allow me to help you."

"I will, I promise," I answer as more tears fall down my cheeks.

LESLIE FEAR

He lets go of my hands and pulls me close. The incredible smell of his skin and the warmth of his body so close to mine is like coming home. I finally have someone else to rely on. I finally have someone who will always have my back.

His lips hover over my ear. "You are my Queen and I will honor you as long as I have breath," he whispers, the heat and sincerity of his words sending goosebumps throughout my body. "Let us make decisions together," he kisses a trail along the side of my neck, "as a team."

"Now, sleep," he orders. His voice is deep and hushed, like he's still caught up in the moment, and I'm pulled out of my lustful thoughts by his choice of words. It's hard to think about resting when I look up and watch his heavy lidded caramel eyes drop down to my lips.

"Can't you stay? At least until I fall asleep?" I whisper.

He shakes his head and moves to stand. "Zack and I must attend to a few things."

"What things?"

Dominic takes in a deep breath and lets it out slowly. "It's nothing you need to worry about now."

"What do you mean, nothing I should worry about...*now*?"

"Never mind, Kate," he says. "Sleep. We will discuss everything with you in the morning."

"Yeah, yeah." I have to catch myself from rolling my eyes. "You and Zack keep telling me that," I remind him, my frustration starting to build, "but the truth is, neither one of you has told me much of anything this entire time."

"It is not that simple," Dominic begins, pacing. "The process takes time. There are rules and traditions—but most of all, there is honor." He stops and locks eyes with me. "We all have a duty to protect the realm."

"Realm?" I ask as new questions start swirling around in my head. "It would seriously be nice if someone would finally clue me in. How am I supposed to understand my place if you don't tell me anything?"

"Now that you have transitioned, it *is* time."

"Good. Start talking."

"I must go, but I will discuss more with you tomorrow morning, when you will be presented before the Seraph Council." His expression becomes more intense. "The council is something you will soon be quite acquainted with."

Gulp.

I look around the room for my clothes, itching to go with him, to learn more. "That sounds pretty important."

Dominic smiles and takes my hand. He tucks the blankets in around me and I know he can already feel my apprehension. "Do not worry, you will have everything you need after you rest." His face brightens. "And you will also have an assistant to help you with the proper dress and etiquette."

"What?" I laugh. "Like a lady-in-waiting?"

"Something very similar to that, I imagine. Her name is Victoria and she has been with me..." He instantly stops himself. He probably didn't mean to say the "me" part. "She is one of many Seraph Followers who assist our leaders."

"What do you mean, she's been with you?" I blurt out, not even hearing the rest of what he just said. "Near you in the castle or 'with you' with you?"

His brow furrows and I can tell there's something between them. I try like hell not to think the worst but it's impossible. She's probably gorgeous and perfect and obedient too. I bet she never rushes headlong into anything or makes impulsive, stupid decisions.

Dominic kisses my forehead. "Sleep, my Queen. All will be clearer in the morning."

When the door opens, a young, beautiful woman looks up at him with a smile. I watch with relief as he walks past her without interacting. The door gently closes and my mind overloads again with questions. Who is she? And, was she actually waiting for him? It sure seemed that way. Is she Victoria, the woman who has been "with him"? Is she someone else entirely? Another admirer?

Shit, it's going to be a long night...

CHAPTER THIRTY

WITHOUT WARNING, THE thick curtains flash apart, daylight flooding the room. I open my eyes blearily, finally making out a petite, light-haired woman. Her hands are loaded and she darts from one side of the room to another, picking things up and setting things down.

I spent hours last night letting my thoughts torture me about some chick Dominic may or may not have had a thing with and hopefully, I'll get some answers from him today. Right now I'm just plain exhausted and not in any mood to meet new people. "Excuse me," I whisper, my voice still groggy. "Who are you?"

The woman whips around, startled. "Oh! You're awake!" she yelps, bending into a full bow as I awkwardly sit up, gathering the covers to my chest.

"Good morning, your Majesty." She smiles, her amazing blue eyes lighting up.

Holy crap, it's her. The same woman I saw outside my door when Dominic left—and she's even more gorgeous close up.

"My name is Victoria," she says, and her delicate, beautifully shaped brows push together. "Did Dominic not tell you I have been assigned your Follower?"

I barely register the words coming out of her mouth and when she stops talking, I'm scrambling for my own words. "Y-yeah, he—he told me," I get out, shading my eyes because the room is so bright. "It's...it's nice to meet you."

She rises up out of her deep bow and I watch her long, wavy blond hair fall off her shoulder in slow motion, like I'm watching some kind of *Vogue* fashion shoot. She's unbelievably stunning and I'm jealous of her all over again.

"The pleasure is all mine, your highness," she says, her face brightening. "I am here to prepare you for your meeting with the Seraph Council."

She opens the double doors to the armoire and I have to catch my breath. It's fully stocked with shimmering jewelry, strands of pearls, breathtaking beaded gowns, brilliant tiaras dripping in diamonds, and an assortment of high-collared fur capes.

I have no idea my mouth is slightly open until I try to swallow the tickle in my throat.

"Come on." She motions me to come over. "We do not have much time."

I have no words. I obey without thought, throwing my legs over the side of the bed and stumbling across the room.

"You are still weak from saving the Dem—I mean, your uncle," she corrects herself. My eyes narrow, but before I can say anything, she continues. "It is my duty to know everything about your life, your family, and your demeanor."

She smiles and chuckles a little; I have no doubt my expression is the cause. I'm stunned and barely awake and now some stranger has just admitted she knows everything there is to know about my life.

What the...

"I have chosen this one," she holds up a gorgeous full-length, sleeveless, burgundy gown, "for your meeting with the council."

She drapes it over the bed and immediately begins pulling off my nightgown. I shyly fold my arms over my chest. I only have my underwear on at this point and without warning, her arms come up from behind me.

"Lift, please," she instructs and I do, trying not to shiver when she wraps something around my midsection. It's stiff and reaches from my waist all the way to my breasts. Her hand cups one of my shoulders and she starts to gather the strings along my back, yanking them tightly.

"Ouch!" I cry, not meaning to raise my voice as much as I do. "What are you doing?"

"It's called a corset, silly," she jokes. "And you will need to get used to them."

I don't know her well enough to know if she's being funny or sarcastic but I figure I better set the tone of our relationship now instead of later.

"Loosen up the strings, please," I say over my shoulder with more authority than I feel. "I'll need to be able to breathe if I have to talk to a group of strangers."

She stops tugging, loosening the strings and retying them. Almost immediately, I can take a full deep breath.

"Thank you." I exhale as she walks past me and picks up the grown.

"Of course," she says, her tone not nearly as cheerful. "Lift again, please," she instructs, only this time her smile is way less authentic.

Good. Let's not forget who I am, sister.

Lifting my arms, I allow the gown to slip down my body. It fits like a glove. Victoria quickly takes my arm and guides me to the full-length mirror on the inside of the armoire door. My eyes go wide when I see my reflection. The floor length, silk and satin gown is beyond stunning, with scrolled gold and silver beading coming to a point at the center of my chest. I'm so taken aback by the dress that I barely notice the fact that there's hardly a need to fix my hair or apply any makeup. Because of my transition, those things are almost entirely done.

"Oh, your highness," she gives me a curtsy, "you're absolutely breathtaking." The adorning look on her face makes me feel like crap for thinking the worst about her.

"Thank you," I reply, wondering if we got off of the wrong foot.

Her eyes light up at my words and she smiles, proud of the job she's done. Maybe I'm wrong about her. Maybe I need to relax. I'm bad about judging people before they even have a chance to get close to me. I should probably work on that.

But there's still a lingering question I need to ask. What is her connection with Dominic? And do they still have one? This might be a good time to ask a few questions.

"So, how long have you served as a Follower?" I ask, trying to sound as nonchalant as possible.

Victoria stops searching for the perfect earrings to match my dress and looks at me as if I've surprised her. "Oh, um—let me see." Her brow creases like she's calculating. "Seventy-three years."

Wait, what?

I'm at a loss for words because now I'm clearly the one who's surprised. Floored is more like it. Did she really just say seventy-three? Years?

"I don't...wait, that's impossible." I stumble through my thoughts, "You're just messing with me, right?" I manage to smile even though this isn't the least bit humorous. "I mean, you can't be much older than me."

She tilts her head and gets a funny look on her face like she's starting to realize something. "They haven't told you," her brows push together, "have they?"

"Told me what?" I ask, dreading whatever she's referring to. What other secrets haven't I been told?

"Dominic will be here soon." She smiles. "It will be better coming from him."

Holy hell, maybe I really was right. Maybe there actually is something between them. I feel the blood rushing to my face before I can gather my thoughts and suddenly, I don't care what I say or who I offend. "Tell me now!" I shout at her, completely letting go of my emotions.

The huge wooden door to the bedroom flies open with a crash. As if on cue, Dominic rushes in with an urgent look on his face. He's furious.

"Victoria!" he calls. "Leave us!"

Her eyes go up to him, the hurt behind them clearly visible, and she rushes out, stopping to shut the door quietly, looking quietly defeated.

"What did she tell you?" Dominic shouts, and I wonder if he's mad at me too.

"Nothing!" I shout back, frustrated by his tone. "She told me it—whatever *it* is—would be better coming from you!"

His face drops and I can't help wondering if I've told him a totally different story than what he assumed. Without warning, he turns around and storms out the door.

What just happened?

I'm breathing like I just sprinted a marathon and it takes me only a second to realize that Dominic just ran after Victoria, my Follower. The girl I've been insanely jealous of since I learned about her existence. What is it between them? And what else has he *not* told me?

My mind is about to explode with questions as my hands nervously begin rubbing together. Is he coming back? Doesn't he know I'm freaking the hell out? Am I going to have to face the stupid council on my own?

I pause when I catch my reflection in the mirror; it's like looking at a completely different person. Physically, I've changed into a woman. There's no question I've gained some confidence but if I'm being honest, mentally I'm still a scared teenager who doubts herself and everyone around her. And why shouldn't I? Nobody's given me a straight answer about anything and now I'm seriously about to lose my shit.

A slow creak of the opening door jars me out of my thoughts. Zack nods in appreciation, closing it behind him. "We need to talk," he says, walking past me with a look of intense concentration.

"Where's Dominic?" I yell without thinking, and I know he can hear the worry and even the jealousy in my voice.

"He will be here shortly." He pauses, looking at me with his new blue eyes. "It's important to stay calm, Katie."

"Calm? You tell me to stay calm when I wake up to a woman I don't even know rearranging my bedroom like she owns the place?" I take a breath, ready to go on. "Then she tells me she's been a Follower for this place for seventy-three years. She hardly looks older than me. And what is she to—"

"It's a little more complicated than that," he interrupts.

"It always is, Zack!" I shout. "But it doesn't matter right now because you need to tell me what she thought I knew and why she ran out when Dominic barged in." I pause, narrowing my eyes. "I swear to you, if you don't tell me, I won't leave this room and that little council of yours can go straight to hell."

170

Zack's eyes close on my last word and he takes my arm, guiding me to one of the wingback chairs in front of the fireplace. "Sit," he instructs, taking a seat across from me. "This information should be coming from your betrothed, but under the circumstances, I will answer your questions." He swallows and looks miserable, like this is the last discussion he wants to have. "First things first, it's true. Victoria has been with us for a while."

I shift in the chair, trying my best to calm down and let him talk.

"Like you, she is..." he stops as I hang on his every word, "immortal."

I only hear one word.

"Immortal," I repeat. "Like, she can't be killed?"

He chuckles under his breath as if I said something funny. "Well, there are a couple of ways we, as immortals, can die, but essentially, yes."

"Hang on, you said, 'we' so that means," I pause, taking in what he just said, "I am too?"

Zack nods and I can actually feel the blood draining from my face.

Holy shit.

"But-but, how?" I barely get out.

"Your transition," he continues as I attempt to wrap my brain around another round of unbelievable news, "is when it happened."

"That's why Dominic was so upset with Victoria? Because he's the one who's supposed to tell me I'm-I'm immortal?" I ask, trying to piece it together.

He nods.

"But, she didn't," I say, wondering why I'm now defending her. "She didn't tell me anything. Well, nothing I didn't actually ask."

"She almost did, and Dominic picked up on that," Zack explains. "We have rules to abide by." He looks down, rubbing the scruff on his chin. I can tell he already knows what my next question will be. "Dominic and Victoria have a unique connection," he continues, locking eyes with me. "But the rest of their story will have to come from him."

"Zack…" I say in a warning tone and his hands immediately go up.

"Katie, I—I'm serious." He shakes his head. "It's not my place."

Without saying a word, I walk straight toward the door.

"Katie!" Zack calls after me. "Where are you going?"

I ignore him. I'm on a mission to find Dominic as rolling hot lava begins to burn its way through every vein in my body. I've had it. I've finally lost every ounce of patience I had left. Why didn't Dominic explain everything to me up front? What's with all the ridiculous secrecy? Does he think I can't handle it?

The torch-lit corridor is cold, but I hardly notice. My four-inch heels amplify my rising temper as they echo off the stone walls. Several people stop to bow or curtsy as I rush by on my quest to find or maybe, catch the two little lovebirds. The hallways seem to multiply; it's confusing to know which way to go and I wish like hell I'd paid more attention or at least someone had shown me around before now.

"Your Majesty." A man in a brown cloak catches my eye, stepping to the side of the hallway to bow.

I smile, as something catches my attention and I look past him. It sounds like low conversation and it's getting louder the closer I get to the end of the hall. Maybe it's him. Maybe it's both of them doing God knows what. I stop just outside the door, my body beginning to tremble. I'm startled when a hand gently takes my arm. I whip my head over my shoulder to see the familiar black cloak shrouding the man I love. He pulls me with him into a room across the hall, shutting the door quietly before glaring down at me.

"Why are you without a chaperone?" His tone is low and heated.

Hold up, he doesn't get to be mad.

"What?" I whisper-shout, pointing my finger at his chest. "*You* left *our* room without a word or explanation to chase after a woman you're clearly *involved* with and you're pissed off at me?"

Dominic's brows push together and he scans the room like someone might be spying on us. His eyes narrow back at me. "It is not the time or the place to have this conversation."

"Seriously?" I shout, placing my hands on my hips. "When will it be the right time or place, Dominic? Never? Because all the secrets, all the things I still don't know... They're exactly why I'm about to lose it!" I pause to take a breath. "I get nothing, no explanation, nada! I'm starting to feel like a God-damned hostage!"

"Lower your voice!" he growls in a whisper so close to my face, I almost forget how upset I am. "This place, our Realm," his eyes move around the room, "is sacred and there is no tolerance for schoolgirl drama."

He did NOT just say that.

I take in another full, deep breath, attempting to calm myself, but change my mind and decide to let him have it. "You don't want drama? You don't want my immature schoolgirl bullshit? Fantastic, because I'm done! You can have your precious little girlfriend and her perfect freaking petite body and everything else in this Godforsaken place and shove it straight up your ass!" I say, managing to keep my voice under the shouting threshold.

His jaw tightens as I speak, my eyes dropping down to his lips as they slowly curl into a mischievous smile. "You think Victoria and I are…" He laughs like I've told him the funniest joke on the planet.

"What's so funny?" I ask, trying like hell to keep from smiling because it's true what they say about genuine laughter. It's contagious.

He pulls me close. God, he smells so good. I try to wiggle my way free, remembering how furious I am, or was, but he tightens his hold as his soft lips touch my ear.

"You are mine. You will always be mine. And trust me, you have absolutely nothing to worry about."

CHAPTER THIRTY-ONE

RELIEF WASHES OVER me like a stream of warm water as Dominic's huge arms wrap around my waist. Closing my eyes, I take in the feel of his body so close to mine, almost forgetting that I was beyond angry only seconds ago.

Wait a minute.

"So, I need to know." My voice cracks a little. "Are you going to tell me who Victoria really is? Or is that a secret, too?" I whisper, trying to keep my emotions in check this time.

He takes a second to answer and I wonder if he's deciding how much to say. The needles are back, poking around in my gut. "She has been a trusted friend," he pulls back and his eyes go soft when he looks at me, "for a very long time."

"Yeah," I reply, swallowing hard, "she mentioned something about that." I stop, hoping he'll fill in more of the blanks but he stays quiet, so I repeat her words. "Seventy-three years, right?"

His eyes wrinkle slightly at the corners. I can tell he's not happy I know that part. "Yes, and I haven't spoken to her about boundaries yet. I wanted to ease you into this process." He strokes my hair. "New arrivals to the Realm don't happen often. It is all new to her, too." He looks away.

"Why didn't you tell me?" I wait for his gaze to come back to me. "Why didn't you just tell me that...that I'm immortal?"

"Your reaction confirms what I knew would happen. You were not ready." He gently tilts his head. "Like I said, you need time to adjust. There is a process we must abide by."

"Oh." I stop to think for a second. "So, why didn't Victoria know that? Why would she blurt things out that you weren't ready for me to know? How can you be so trusting of her?"

He shakes his head a little like he's not sure either. "This is all new to her." His lips press together. "But I think she might feel somewhat threatened by you."

"Why? Aren't you just friends?" I air quote the 'just' part.

"Yes, but..." his expression changes like it's hard for him to talk about, "she has always wanted more from me than I could offer." His words come out in a whisper but I know he's telling me the truth.

Now we're getting somewhere.

"So you're saying she wanted you two to be more than friends?"

Dominic closes his eyes and I know I've hit that nail on the head.

"Well, that explains everything," I say, louder than I should have. "Glad you sent someone you *trust* to coach me." I allow the sarcasm to hang in the air.

"I do not think of her in that way—I never have," he says, his tone slightly defensive. "But I stand by my decision. You can trust her and she will guide you better than any other Follower in the Realm."

I shake my head, wondering if I can do this with a woman who wishes she had the man I love—and probably has for over seventy years. How can I compete with that? She must know everything there is to know about Dominic.

"It is not a competition," he says, reading my mind. "Victoria knows where I stand and has for years but she *can* be... protective."

My eyes instantly go to his. "You think?"

He smiles again and pulls me close. "I have already spoken to her and she understands that you will not threaten the friendship she and I have had all these years."

"Good, because I swear, Dominic, I can't take any more secrets." I look up into his beautiful multi-colored eyes and know, without a doubt, that he's sincere—but there's still another question I want to ask.

"D-do I need to be scared?" I rest my forehead on his chest. "Is the Seraph Council going to reprimand me or something for saving Uncle John?"

"No." His finger goes to my chin and he gently pulls up. "What you choose to do is neither right nor wrong in their eyes. They will advise you on how to handle your uncle, but for now, they are more concerned about something else. Or I should say, someone else."

"Someone else?" I let the words fly out of my mouth before he finishes. "Who? Aunt Kelly?"

"No." His face changes and I can almost feel the seriousness behind his eyes. "Skylar."

"Huh? Why?" I ask, wondering what he has to do with anything. I haven't seen him since he and Zack sent him home from the cave. I haven't even checked my phone for messages for that matter.

"The Council will discuss everything with you." He stops and takes both of my hands. "But they know where he is."

"Who, the Council?" I ask. "Why would they care where Skylar is?"

Dominic's lips tighten and I know it's hard for him to tell me. He squeezes my hands. "Not the Council," he says, and his eyes glow slightly red, "the Demons."

"What would the Demons want with—" I stop and look away because it's all coming clear. I glance back up to Dominic and he nods. He knows what I'm thinking.

"They're after me," I say, closing my eyes as I take in a quick breath. "And they'll do anything to get to me—even if they have to hurt my best friend."

"Yes, so we must act quickly." His hands cup my face. "The Council is waiting," He leans in and kisses the top of my head. "Are you ready?"

"I think so. Will you hold my hand?" I ask as a single tear falls down my cheek.

He wipes it away with his thumb and his face goes soft. "Anything you wish, my Queen."

Reaching over my shoulder, he gently opens the door, slipping his fingers through mine as he takes the lead. "Follow me. It is not far."

The dimly lit hallway is quiet and completely void of people, unlike before. Dominic guides me down another set of hallways just as quiet as the last. I'm a little out of breath because it feels as though we're climbing stairs even though I haven't seen one since we started. After a few minutes, Dominic stops and I can't believe my eyes as I stare in awe at two arched, shimmering gold doors. The intricate carvings of angels and maybe a royal crest are massive and simply stunning. Dominic lets go of my hand and pulls the hood over his head like he's gearing up for battle.

I grab his arm, holding tight. "I'm afraid," I admit, staring into his warm, beautiful eyes.

He takes my hands in his. "There is no need for you to be frightened." He gives me a light smile. "Although, there are some things I should tell you before we go in."

"Okay," I say, trying to keep my stomach from doing flip-flops. "I want to be prepared."

"You must remember your answers are neither right nor wrong. They will know if your words are truthful and of honorable intent," he says, taking in a breath. "This is the most holy place you will ever be."

Gulp.

"It is an honor to be called before the Seraph Council. Remember that." He steps forward and slowly opens the door. "Behold, my Queen," he whispers and bows.

I take one last look into his amazing eyes before taking a step.

The gold carved doors are nothing compared to the inside of the room and I have to catch my breath to hold it together. If someone can be physically punched in the gut by sheer beauty then I've been hit hard. Every single thing is white—the floors, the ceiling, the walls—but it's as if everything is alive somehow, spreading what I can only describe as comfort and reassurance. Billowy white clouds surround my feet and it feels like I'm barely touching the ground, almost as if I'm floating.

"Hello, Katherine Elizabeth," a male voice calls out.

I look straight ahead to see three people in pure white cloaks sitting side by side, fading in and out of more wispy, beautiful clouds. Dominic stops and kneels immediately and I follow suit, shaking the whole way down.

"There is no need to fear us," the male voice says. "We are only here to advise."

I can only nod. Three of them sit together at the other end of the room in pure white cloaks. I'm pretty sure my vocal chords aren't working yet. Dominic slips his fingers in mine, sending a soothing rush through my body. No doubt he's feeling my butterflies too.

"We do not have much time, so let us begin with your uncle," another, deeper male voice says. "What made you feel the need to save his life when he tried many times to take yours?"

I swallow, trying to think of the best answer, but I'm interrupted by another voice. "Do not try to think of the right response, you need only to give us the truthful one."

I take in a deep breath, realizing Dominic was right. They will know if I'm not completely genuine so I give them what they want. "Because I couldn't stand watching Aunt Kelly grieve." I glance down at our intertwined fingers before looking back up. "Even if Uncle John tried to take my life, it wasn't his fault. It was the Demon inside of him."

"So you risked your own life again to save him? Even though you were not certain the Demon was truly gone?" a female voice calls out.

"Y-yes, well, I thought he was back to being Uncle John again." I swallow hard. "Aunt Kelly was hurting and I knew I had the power to do something about it," I answer honestly, hoping it's enough.

Silence follows and I'm back to being scared to death. I can tell they're talking amongst themselves, even through the heavy clouds because I hear whispering. I just can't make out the words.

Eventually, the male on the right says, "We understand and accept your actions."

Dominic squeezes my hand and I smile up at him.

"We have another matter to discuss with you." The first male voice interrupts my small victory. "Your friend, Skylar—he is in danger."

"Yes," I answer, "Dominic told me the Demons have found him."

"We must keep him safe," the female says.

"I agree. But how?" I ask, finally starting to feel a little less nervous.

"We will assign a Warrior to watch over him."

CHAPTER THIRTY-TWO

I GLANCE UP AT Dominic, hoping the Council isn't talking about assigning him as Skylar's Warrior. I'm pretty sure I'd go completely insane if he were gone. Not to mention I don't want to deal with Victoria on my own.

"We have no intention of separating you from one another," the female says, reading my thoughts. "We have accepted and approve of your bond, although Seraph Warrior Dominic will be required to advise and assist the new Warrior when the time arises."

Wait, what?

"Assist?" I ask so quickly I barely realize the words have flown out of my mouth.

"Yes," the male on the left says, nodding. "Seraph Warrior Dominic is our most skilled and qualified fighter."

I glance back to the three Council members as fresh needles poke at my gut. "I…I've seen what these Demons can do. Dominic almost lost his life saving me." My eyes start to tear. "There are many other Warriors in the castle; let them handle the Demons," I practically beg them to keep him out of it.

Dominic loosens his grip on my hand and pulls away. I don't have to be a mind reader to know he's pissed. *Really pissed.*

"This is not your decision," he bites out through the side of his mouth.

"We understand your concern," the male on the left chimes in, "though our decision has been made."

Before I can say another word, the female starts talking. "Seraph Warrior Dominic," she says, and his furious eyes pull away from mine, "the Council has decided to award you three additional crystals. Each will perform to your will at the time of their use. Your bravery and your honor to our new Queen have been most impressive."

Dominic bows his head, ignoring the fact that I'm still staring at him. "The honor is all mine. I will do everything within my power to use them wisely and to protect the Realm," he finally looks over to me, "and my Queen."

"We are pleased to hear it," the female says, then turns to the other Council members. They whisper amongst themselves for a moment, then look up.

The male on the left says, "We have appointed Seraph Warrior Gideon as Skylar Bennett's protector. Seraph Warrior Dominic, please inform and advise him of everything that is required."

"It will be my pleasure," Dominic says as he bows his head again.

"Excellent," the female says, then whispers something to the other Council members. She nods to me next. "Queen Katherine Elizabeth." Her face is shadowed by the hood of her cloak but I can tell she wants my full attention. "Every decision you make within the Realm must be accompanied with pure intent. The responsibilities you now have as our Queen depend on your wise and thoughtful judgment."

I nod, swallowing so hard I'm pretty sure everyone heard it and drop down into a bow in acknowledgement.

"As you grow to know the Realm," the female voice continues, "you will begin to understand our advice and how vital your actions will be. First you must let go of the life you once had, so that you may accept the one you have been rightfully given."

Before I have time to think, the wispy clouds surrounding them suddenly thicken up, curling around in waves and completely shrouding the Council members until they're no longer visible.

"We must go," Dominic says.

I pull myself up to stand, turning to follow him through the now open golden doors. The second we cross the threshold they automatically close and my eyes quickly readjust to the dimly lit hallways. Dominic is ahead of me and I practically have to run to catch up to him. Reaching out to touch his arm, I manage to grab part of his cloak but he keeps going.

"Dominic, wait!" I call to him.

He flashes around to me and I swear the wind from his cloak moves my dress. "I am a Warrior!" he whisper-shouts. "I have always been a Warrior and I will not allow you to try and persuade the Council to keep me from my duties. Or my honor."

Holy crap.

"I...I only..."

"You may be my Queen, but I decide who, when, and how I fight."

I watch Dominic's eyes shift from brownish red to a deeper combination of the two. I don't know what to do or even say. He's clearly still livid with me and I'm not sure if it's because I asked the Council not to have him advise Gideon or not to let him fight. Either way, it doesn't matter now because I need to fix this.

"I'm sorry!" I blurt out, reaching up to touch his arm. "I just want you to stay with me," I say, my voice falling into a whisper. "I want to know you're safe."

He's still breathing heavy but something I said or did must have worked because he's no longer trying to get away from me. He's actually listening. "I am a Warrior first," he says, his voice much calmer than before. "Everything else in my life is second."

His words practically punch me in the stomach and I have to take in a quick breath. What am I doing, falling in love with a man who can't, and from what it sounds won't, put me first?

"You do not understand," he says in response to the thoughts running through my head. "The Realm, the Seraph Council, fighting Demons to keep everyone safe, especially you—all of that has to come first."

When you put it that way...

Dominic pulls back and takes me by the shoulders. "Since I was a young boy, I knew I was a Warrior—a fighter for good." His eyes drift off like he's reliving a memory. "Once I transitioned, defending the Realm is all I have ever known." He looks back down to me and his two last words come out deep and hushed. "Until you."

"So hang on, you've always just trained to be a Warrior?" I clear my throat. "You've never dated or you know, had a relationship with a woman?" I look away, embarrassed that I even allowed the words to come out of my mouth.

His expression softens even more. "My attention has been diverted a time or two." He grins, enjoying teasing me. "Although, nothing more. You must understand, Seraph Warriors mate for life and I knew pretty quickly when a woman was not right for me." He cups my cheek in his palm. "I knew better so I never let things go too far."

"None of *them*?" I interrupt, instantly wishing I would just keep my big mouth shut.

"Kate, I have been here for seventy-six years."

Oh my God, that's right.

"So, you've never...?" I regret my words the second they come out of my mouth.

His face becomes a little more serious. "If you are asking if I am a virgin," he pauses for a second, "the answer is no." His hand slips from my face and he looks away.

"I...I'm sorry. I shouldn't have asked." I reach up to touch his arm and his eyes come back to me.

"It is something I regret every day," he says, his voice barely a whisper.

"Why?"

"Because it went against everything I was taught, everything that I am."

"Dominic, come on. You've been here for a long time." I shake my head. "I'm surprised it only happened once."

He lets out a deep breath. "I think it is part of the reason I thought of myself as a Warrior above anything else."

I can tell this is a difficult conversation for him and if I'm being honest, I really don't want to hear any more about his past girlfriends.

Except.

"What about Victoria?" I ask, hoping he'll tell me what I want to know. "Was she the one..."

He shakes his head again. "She was different," he admits. "I never thought of her in that way and I do not know why, but I am grateful for it now." The corners of his eyes wrinkle slightly, "I knew pretty quickly that I could trust her, even though I was

186

aware that she wanted more from me." He scans the hallway before continuing. "And I was careful not to be cruel about it; she was and still is extremely sensitive. But from the beginning, Victoria has always been like a sister to me."

"So, that's why you ran after her?" I ask, knowing it's a rhetorical question.

Dominic nods and closes his eyes for a second. "She means a lot to me and I never want to hurt her," he admits, staring into my eyes. "I love her, Kate." He leans down and gently kisses my lips. "But it is not the same kind of love I have for you."

Wow...

If mere words can actually make someone fall deeper in love, then Dominic just succeeded. The unveiled honesty behind his eyes alone is enough to make me melt into a puddle, right here, right now.

Without hesitation, I pull him into a hug and sigh at the feeling of his arms wrapping around my waist. Tears are already welling up my vision and I'm not sure I could be more grateful for him than I am at this very moment. This is where I'm supposed to be and it's clearer than ever before that he is my destiny. In his arms it finally feels like I'm home.

CHAPTER THIRTY-THREE

DOMINIC TAKES MY hand in his and kisses it as we walk down the hallway together. I can't stop looking up into his amazing eyes when I hear someone approaching. Dominic turns his head in the direction of the heavy footsteps but it only takes another second for me to recognize my brother's walk. The expression on his face is serious and he hasn't looked at me once. His eyes are only directed at Dominic, and I can tell something's up.

"Gideon is waiting for you in the Great Hall." Zack finally looks away from Dominic and acknowledges me with a slight nod.

"On my way." Dominic kisses the side of my face turning in the same direction Zack came from and I pull his arm back.

"Hang on. Don't we," I look back up at him, "get *any* time to ourselves?"

Zack sighs under his breath, as if he's a little annoyed, and my eyes go straight to his. "Katie, time is of the essence. Skylar needs our immediate protection."

"I-I get that, but—"

"Kate," Dominic stops my words, "Zack is right. I must go." He gently pulls away and shifts his eyes back to Zack. "Escort her back to our quarters. I will not be long."

He takes off, his black cloak obediently swaying behind his large frame as he disappears down the dark hallway. Zack taps my shoulder, diverting my attention and holds out his elbow, so I take it as a question pops in my head.

"Why doesn't Dominic call you "Master" anymore?" I ask as we begin walking.

Zack shakes his head and smiles slightly like it's obvious. "He was merely calling me by my rightful title, just as 'Warrior' is his. That is all," he answers, keeping us at a steady pace.

"And what exactly does a Master do?"

He sighs again, apparently not surprised I asked. "That's a difficult question to answer." He stops so we're both standing in the middle of the hallway. "First and foremost, I work in close liaison with the Seraph Council. They depend on me to keep the Realm safe, especially when it comes to accepting outsiders or I should say, 'non-Seraph' beings as needed for medical and general workings within the castle."

"So you're like a manager?" I smile, teasing him with my choice of word. He chuckles, shaking his head. "Yeah, I guess you could say that."

"H-how did it happen, Zack?" My eyes fall away from his, finally asking the question I've been meaning to ask him this whole time. "How did you come back?"

His brows push together and he takes in a deep breath. "I'm not exactly sure, honestly. One day I was a fighting fires and the next, I was standing before the Seraph Council, talking to them about what my duties were. At least that's how I remember it. I was scared to death, just like you, but they took time to mentor me, making sure I understood what was going on—and that being here was because of our family lineage." He squeezes my hand. "Exactly like it is for you."

"But that's just it," I quickly get out, "what are my duties? And why are the Demons specifically after me?"

"Your duties are similar to mine, keeping the Realm safe." He looks past me and around, like he's making sure no one's walking by. "The Demons know you can destroy them, don't you see that? And any threat to them is a threat right back to us."

Gulp.

"Dominic can kill them."

"Yes, but he can't bring back life. You can."

I shake my head because again, I have more questions than answers, "Okay, so how can I do more than just getting rid of them? How can I actually kill a Demon?"

"That hasn't been revealed yet, but the Council has told me that our most powerful abilities will come in time. Just like your other abilities have." He offers his elbow again. "So, in the meantime, we have to keep you safe."

I slip my hand through his arm. "If this place is so safe, why do I need an escort?"

He closes his eyes for a second and smiles, like this answer is obvious, too. "You are our Queen. It is proper and expected for you to have someone by your side at all times—especially when you're in public." He pats my hand as we continue walking side by side.

We pass several Fighters who stop and bow as soon as they notice me. I smile and nod, wondering if I'll ever get used to this when we finally make it to my room. Zack opens the door to find Victoria hanging a new dress in the armoire.

"Your Majesty," she bends into a deep bow, "can I get you some something? Food or maybe something to drink?" she asks as if the drama from earlier never happened.

Now that you mention it.

"Um, yeah." I'd actually kill for some carbonation right now. "Can I get a Diet Coke?"

She glances over to Zack and then back to me. "Of course, anything you wish." She smiles and darts out of the room and I instantly wonder how long it'll be awkward between us. I can't worry about that now. I've got so many questions I don't even know where to start.

I catch Zack watching Victoria leave before he moves to one of the wingbacks. He clearly wants privacy so when he takes a seat, I take advantage of the moment.

"Uncle John..." I lock eyes with him before getting the words out, hoping, no praying, I didn't make the biggest mistake ever. "How is he?"

Zack's expression changes and I'm not sure if he's troubled or just trying to hide something. "He's doing okay, I suppose." He rubs his hands together. "But I'm concerned about him."

He looks away like he's slightly hesitant to tell me more. "Uncle John is for sure extremely angry," Zack admits, and his eyes come back to me. "Honestly, it's difficult to know if there's still a Demon attached to him or not." He shifts and leans forward, resting his elbows on his knees. "I mean, obviously, he's tormented by the loss of his hand."

Oh crap, I forgot about that.

"Maybe I should go talk to—"

"No!" Zack interrupts. "We cannot allow that, not again. He's not in the state of mind to speak with you—or Dominic."

Shit.

"W-what about Aunt Kelly? Can't she help?" I begin to pace back and forth. "Isn't there anyone in this place who can tell us what's going on with him for sure?"

"Yes," he whispers, and I'm getting a weird vibe from his tone.

"Okay, then let's find out. Who can tell us?"

Zack locks eyes with me and my stomach immediately drops.

"Oh, no, no." I start pacing again. "I can't do it." I shake my head. "You saw how badly I handled that whole situation. I had no idea what I was even doing!" I raise my voice without thinking.

Zack gets up from his chair and reaches out, taking me by the shoulders with both hands. "Just as we've discussed, your gifts reach way beyond your ability to teleport or even to save a life. I want you to think back to the moment you decided to save Uncle John. Why did you save him?"

"Why does everyone keep asking me that question?" I blurt out. "I did it for Aunt Kelly!"

"Yes, but would you have done it had you known the Demon was still inside him?"

"That's just it, I didn't know," I whisper, looking away. "Well, not for sure, anyway."

"Yes, you did. When you saved his life, you also saw into his soul—which is why you collapsed afterward. You made the Demon leave his body. Dominic and I both watched it." His new blue eyes get serious when I look up, "Even though it was incredibly risky and you could have died."

"I know, I know, I have to use better judgment, I get that now. But hang on, you're not saying I'm going to have to lip-lock our uncle again to know the truth?"

"No," he replies and I let out a thankful breath, "all you have to do is spend a few minutes with him—look into his eyes, maybe ask him a question."

"Seriously, Zack? Anyone can do that." I roll my eyes.

"True, but not everyone has the gift of discernment. And I know for a fact that you do."

I take a seat across from him. "Discernment, huh? I thought you said he was too unstable for me to be around him."

"He is, but there's another way," my brother admits, his expression becoming serious again. "We will have to make Aunt Kelly agree to it, though." He rubs his jaw. "We will also need to have a couple of Warriors holding him down to keep him from attacking you."

Holy crap.

I stand up because I can feel my body start to tremble. "So let me get this straight. I may have gotten rid of the Demon when I brought him back, but there's a good chance it's returned?"

"It's rare, but yes—and this Demon could be particularly evil."

"Wait a second." I turn my face to the side but I'm still looking him dead on, "W-what *exactly* do you mean? How particularly evil? Is there an evilness scale?"

"Let's just say that if Satan himself had sidekicks, this Demon would be one of them."

The look on my face must have engaged Zack's brotherly instincts because he instantly rushes to me, grabbing my arms to keep me from falling flat on my ass.

"Oh, no. I...I'm not ready for this," I get out, as Zack pulls me back down to the wingback.

"Actually, you are." Zack squats in front of me like I'm a child. "You've already dealt with him once. I'm confident you can do it again." He smiles but it's the kind that's riddled with caution.

"You and Dominic did it, not me!" I whisper-shout, trying to catch a full breath.

"That's where you're wrong." He takes my hands. "We only weakened the Demon. You were the one who removed him completely."

"Then why is he back?" I close my eyes for a second. "H-how is he back?"

Zack bites one side of his lip. "Like I said, your more powerful abilities will develop over time and this Demon, or I should say, Zull, is particularly bad and obviously extremely powerful." He lets out a breath before going on. "Most Demons don't have the strength to fight against even one Seraph, let alone three of us, all at once. I knew then that there would be a good chance Zull would return."

"So you think he's back?"

Zack's lips tighten and he nods, suddenly looking past me as the sound of quick footsteps approach us, echoing off the stone floor.

"Here you are, your Majesty." Victoria smiles, handing me a glass filled with ice and the Diet Coke I requested.

"Thank you." I take it from the tray she's holding like she's become some kind of waitress.

Zack pulls his eyes from her and looks back to me. I can tell he wants to continue our discussion privately.

"I'll only be a minute," I say and thank God, she clues in and rushes out the door before I have to ask her to leave. I don't need more awkwardness between the two of us.

As soon as she closes the door, Zack stands and walks to the fireplace, propping his elbow on the mantle. "So," he sighs, "the next thing to do is talk some sense into Aunt Kelly. She's become extremely protective of him. She barely lets him out of her sight as it is."

"Wait a second, I'm not all that convinced that this is such great idea."

He looks at me like he can't believe what I just said. "You underestimate yourself, Katie."

"And how is that?" I blurt out. "I mean, c'mon, Zack. I saved our uncle's life, against your wishes, and he still might be possessed by a Demon." I shake my head. "My confidence isn't exactly high right now."

"But that's exactly it, Katie!" Zack raises his voice. "You instinctively knew you could breathe life into him." He moves closer to me. "Don't you think that if you even sensed the presence of a Demon you would have stopped yourself?"

I shrug my shoulders. "Maybe. I don't know."

"You need to start trusting your instincts more. You have the ability to do so much more." His new blue eyes practically glowing. "I mean it, Katie, if you sincerely tune into them, your feelings will guide you."

"I wish I had half the confidence in them that you do. I mean, what if I make another mistake, Zack, then what?"

"The only mistakes we make are the ones that are self-serving," he whispers.

"What do you mean?"

"Just that." He looks me in the eyes. "Mistakes happen only if we are guided by our own will without the consideration of others."

"Aunt Kelly," I whisper. "I only brought Uncle John back for her."

Zack smiles proudly; I'm finally getting it.

"Okay," my finger taps my chin, "let's pretend I can do all the things you say I can and we somehow convince Aunt Kelly to let me talk to him—"

"That won't be easy," he chimes in.

"Is she seriously being that difficult?"

"To say the least, yeah." Zack rubs his jaw. "She wants nothing to do with finding out if the Demon is gone for sure, but it's pretty obvious she simply doesn't want to lose him—*again*.

"Okay. So what do you want me to do?" I ask, already pretty sure of his answer and dreading his words before they even come out of his mouth.

"I want you to convince her, of course," he says and I close my eyes. The last thing I want to do is torment her with the possibility of Uncle John experiencing more physical pain...or even death.

"Why can't you talk to her? She'll listen to you—hell, she adores you."

"You know I've already tried, Katie."

"And if I decide against it—what then?"

"He'll die for sure. At least with your help, Uncle John stands a chance."

CHAPTER THIRTY-FOUR

"I WAS AFRAID YOU were gonna say that." I look down, wondering if I can go through this again. It's not like Uncle John's been a standup guy. The asshole did make several passes at me and I never told Aunt Kelly—there's no way I could break her heart with that kind of information. Thank God he was always too drunk to get any further than a forced kiss or a grab at my boob. Otherwise, I'm not sure I could have stopped him. The more I think about it, the more I don't want to help him at all. Maybe Aunt Kelly would be better off with him dead. He's never been a good husband and there's no telling how low he had to sink to meet a Demon in the first place or how long it's been going on. Which brings me to the million dollar question...

"How did he even get involved with a Demon, anyway?"

"It's hard to say," he says, leaning against the mantle. He scratches his forehead. "He's always been kind of a jerk."

"Well, duh—" I say with such disgust he instantly looks over to me.

"What?" He narrows his eyes and I can practically see the wheels turning in his head. "What are you not telling me?"

"Nothing!" I blurt out, but Zack knows I'm hiding something. My quick reaction was a dead giveaway and now I can't even look him in the eyes.

Shit, shit, shit!

"Did he hurt you?" he asks with a fury in his eyes I haven't seen before.

"I...I..."

"Katie!" he shouts, "Did he—?" he stops himself before saying it aloud, somehow figuring things out before I have the courage to tell him.

"No!" I get out. "He...he didn't technically hurt me at all." I close my eyes. "Well, not really."

"Katie," his eyes go wide, "what did he do?" He gets closer to me, reaching over to touch my arm as his anger builds.

I shake my head, pulling away from him, covering my face with my hands. I'm not ready to tell him. It's too painful to think that someone you're supposed to trust, someone who's supposed to love and protect you, could do such a thing. I've held it inside for so long that it feels safer to keep it there, tucked away so no one else can see the ugliness of it.

"That son-of-a-bitch," Zack whispers, walking back toward the mantle as he starts to pace.

I look up, trying to deny his words. "He—I mean, we..." I stop to wipe the tiny rivers already flowing down my face, "It— it never got that far."

"How does that matter?" he shouts, slamming his fist on the mantle. "The fact that he tried—" His fist smashes down again, his other hand racing through his hair. "I'm so sorry, Katie," he says, rushing to my side and lifting me into a tight hug. "I didn't know. Why didn't you tell me?"

I'm not sure if it's because I sometimes felt responsible or the fact that it's finally out in the open, but now, I'm crying on my brother's shoulder like a little girl.

"I couldn't tell you. I couldn't tell anyone." I hiccup.

"How long?" Zack's voice is only a whisper. I can tell he's trying to be careful with his words and I cry a little harder.

"I'm…I'm not sure. Maybe a few months?" I barely get the last word out and feel the wetness from my tears on Zack's white shirt. "He only came in my room when he was drunk but I tried to be nice anyway. I didn't want to make a big deal of it. I didn't want to make things worse for Aunt Kelly."

"I want to kill him myself." He bites out his words, still holding me as I continue to sob. "But it makes more sense now," he whispers after a few moments. "The more corrupt the person, the easier it is for a Demon to manipulate."

I pull back, wondering what he means. "How?" I sniff, wiping away more tears.

Zack lets go but keeps my hand in his. "Uncle John and I have never gotten along, you know that. With me he seemed to always have a chip on his shoulder, like he resented my success or something. I always knew Aunt Kelly was way too good for him." He guides me over to the wingback and I take a seat. "When his drinking got worse and he kept going out at night, I knew he was headed for serious trouble."

"So you're saying the more screwed up a person is, the easier it is for a Demon to possess them?"

"That's exactly what I'm saying."

Zack resumes his spot by the mantle and turns to face me. "You know," he begins, "if we, I mean, you, determine that Zull is still controlling Uncle John, we just might be able to get some valuable information out of him."

"What do you mean?"

199

"We might be able find out what these Demons are up to."

"Isn't that pretty clear? They're after me."

Zack scratches behind his neck. "True, but if we could get Zull to talk about what they know concerning you or Skylar, and how they're planning their strategies—"

"You think Demons seriously care about strategies?" I interrupt.

"I'm pretty sure they're capable of a lot more than we think—including planning some kind of attack."

My stomach drops because the first person I think of is Dominic and how that would most likely involve him. Hell, he'd be the one leading the Warriors straight into battle.

"Theoretically, of course," Zack finishes his thought.

"Okay, I mean, yeah, it would be good to know if they're planning something. Especially if it can help Skylar."

"Exactly. We have to stay one step ahead of them. It's imperative." He rubs his jaw. "And getting inside the head of one of the most evil Demons out there could be a huge advantage for us."

A slow creak from the other side of the room echoes off the stone walls. I see his black cloak before I see his face, whipping around his body like a second skin—it's almost embarrassing that I'm fangirling over him like he's some kind of hot rock star.

"Excellent, I'm glad you're here," Zack says, gesturing him to join us. "Come, sit down."

I knew, but I guess I didn't realize just how intense our mental bond was because I can feel Dominic's urgency. It's practically oozing from his pores—something's definitely up.

"What?" I ask without thinking.

"The situation with Skylar is worse than we thought," he says. I notice the hint of red in his eyes is more prominent now.

"What do you mean?" Zack immediately chimes in.

"Apparently the Demons have been tracking Skylar since he came to the cemetery to find Kate." He nods to me. "He has no recollection of it but unfortunately, he left a trail for them."

My heart starts to pound. "I thought you said he was safe?" I glare at my brother as goosebumps rush down my arms.

"Wait." Zack shakes his head, ignoring my last comment. "How did you find out?"

Dominic's eyes shift from me to Zack. "Two days ago, the Council decided to watch Skylar, mostly because they were concerned the Demons might have locked in on his scent," he looks back at me, "so they sent a Fighter to evaluate the situation. Their suspicions were correct."

"Dammit," Zack says under his breath.

"There is more." Dominic pulls back his hood. "While I was preparing Gideon for his duties, the Fighter returned, informing us that there are several Demons surrounding Skylar's house."

Oh shit!

"How many?" my brother instantly rises from his chair.

"Three, but there could be more," Dominic says.

My stomach practically leaps to my throat. He'll have to go and fight—if my heart could make a noise, they both would have heard a loud scream. Not only is my friend in danger, but the man I love could be too—and it's all because of me.

"We may need to speak to the Council again and request permission to assign more Warriors," Dominic says.

"Does that mean you won't have to go?" I blurt out.

He closes his eyes and I feel like I want to throw up. He's the best Warrior in the Realm, of course he'll be there.

"I am sorry, my love." He kneels down in front of my chair, reaching for my hands. "Even if I had a choice I would still choose to fight."

CHAPTER THIRTY-FIVE

I'M NOT SURE if it's the expression on my face or if he's feeling my anxiety, but Dominic looks past me to Zack and says, "We need a few minutes," his voice almost a whisper. Footsteps, followed by the gentle click of the latch, confirm we're alone as he reaches up and cups my face. "You need to trust me, Kate. I have no intention of dying now, or anytime soon."

I blink, spilling new tears down my cheeks. I have to hold in a sigh when he wipes them away with his thumb. "It's my fault that you have to go at all," I whisper. "I'm so sorry."

"If I have to fight, it should be for the woman I love," he says, his voice hushed.

I reach out, pulling him into a hug as his huge arms wrap around my waist. "I'm so afraid for Skylar. What if—what if…"

"I will keep him safe," Dominic whispers in my ear. "You have my word."

"That's just it. I don't doubt you at all. I…I doubt those bastard Demons, watching his every move."

Dominic pulls away, his expression serious. "That is why it is so urgent to act now," he pauses to wipe another tear under my eye, "so we can prepare before they attempt to take him."

"Holy...take—take him where?" I ask, not really wanting to know. I'm already nauseated just thinking about the possibilities.

"They will try to remove him from his environment and take him into theirs." His caring tone is riddled with caution and I can't help the shiver that creeps up my back.

I swallow, trying not to think about the bile churning in my gut. "W-where would they take him?"

His eyes pull away and he whispers. "Somewhere..." he trails off. "Somewhere we can never allow him to go."

Holy...

"W-w-wait, are you—" I stumble over my words because I'm pretty sure I know the answer. "Do you mean like—like, Hell?"

Dominic nods slightly, making me realize something and I respond without thinking. "Oh my God, hang on, are you telling me that Uncle John—"

"Yes," he interrupts, "And once they go, there is virtually no hope."

I don't have to say a word because he already knows my next question.

"There is only one way a soul can be saved once they enter the depths of Hell," he says, dropping his hands from my waist. "They must want to be delivered from the darkness more than they want to live." His face brightens a little. "That is when you will know if there is a shred of goodness left inside."

"And that's what I'll have to figure out when I talk to Uncle John." I whisper, a feeling of dread washing over me. The last thing I want to do is face that horrible Demon who seemed to know so much about my life.

"If he has been fully immersed in the darkness, your uncle will have no recollection of love, only power and hate."

I let out a breath. "Hopefully I can tell the difference before it's too late."

"You have the gift of discernment," he says, running a finger down my neck. "Like a Seer, if you will. Your abilities are more powerful than you realize."

His voice is low and hushed and instinctively, I take his face in my hands and kiss him harder than I've kissed him ever before. I feel his arms wrap around me as the slight wind from his cloak breezes back my hair. His delicious mouth moves with mine as his lips, his tongue and the feel of his warm body against mine completely intoxicate me. I press harder against him, allowing my mind to escape. I'm in total bliss and so close to ripping off my clothes when suddenly, he pulls back and I let out a whimper.

"You have no idea how hard it is for me to stop," he whispers, his eyes hooded and the perfect mix of reddish-brown. "But we must stay focused for now, my love."

I close my eyes, pulling in a deep breath of his rosemary skin and suddenly, I don't care what lies ahead. If this is how I'll feel every time we get close, I can face anything. I smile and look up, still mesmerized by his incredible eyes. "Then it looks like we have some ass kicking to do."

Dominic chuckles under his breath. "Not so fast," he squeezes my hand, "we are expected at dinner."

My brows automatically push together because this is something new. "Wait, we're not having it here?"

"No, not this time—I would like you to meet someone." His face gets serious again. "Someone I am sure will have questions about Skylar."

Gulp.

"Okay, but I'm not sure how much I can eat."

"You must learn to ignore your concerns and try. You will need to keep up your strength," he says, letting go of my hands as he walks toward the door. "Victoria will assist you," he instructs as she walks in, "and I will meet you outside the banquet hall in fifteen minutes."

What the hell? Was she standing outside listening for her cue or something?

"I know just the thing, Your Highness." She drops to a quick curtsy and rushes over to the armoire, pulling out a gold beaded gown with embroidered flowers cascading down one side. "Yes, I think this will do nicely."

I look over to Dominic, who's already headed out the door; our eyes catch and he gives me a slight nod before walking out.

I think he actually enjoyed that.

"Your Majesty?" Victoria comes up behind me, startling me out of my thoughts. "We do not have much time."

She's holding up the gown and I have to admit, it's stunning. "Yes, of course, thank you." I hold up my arms up as she pulls off the dress I had on, placing it on the bed, and then slips the new dress down my body. I know there's no reason to be upset with her or her connection with Dominic. I understand that he doesn't see her that way, but I'm still a little envious of their long history together

"And here you are." Victoria shows me two sparkling, yellow diamond, tear-drop earrings. "These will go perfectly."

She smiles up at me as I put them on. She's right. They're perfect. So are the darn shoes. She's definitely good at what she does. I'll give her that.

"You look amazing, Your Highness." She smiles, standing back to admire her work. She means it, and I feel the awkwardness between us slipping away.

"Now, just a couple more things," she guides me to the bathroom. I take a seat at the vanity table and watch her perform a quick touch up of my makeup. She then runs a brush through my long, wavy hair a few times, taking the sides and clipping them in a gold barrette before rushing me out the door.

She takes my hand, placing it through her arm. "Okay, let's go find Dominic."

People are everywhere, scattered along the hallway or in groups as if they were waiting for me to make an appearance. Every single person immediately kneels down. I'm still not used to it, trying to remember to nod in acknowledgement of each and every person as I walk by. Thankfully, it doesn't take long before I see the familiar cloak, and the man in it, just outside another set of beautifully carved double doors. I see him take in a breath and bow as I approach.

"Your Majesty," he says in a low, almost seductive voice and if I could jump him right here I would. He rises, extending his left arm, and I take it, trying to hide my arousal. "You are a vision," he whispers, placing his hand over mine. "Are you ready?"

His eyes are instantly comforting, giving off a feeling of reassurance as we walk together into the room. The heavy sound of chairs scooting away from a table startles me as everyone stands at once.

There have got to be at least thirty oversized men in mostly brown cloaks but some are in black but I don't see Zack.

Dominic guides me to the middle of the table, escorting me to the only high back chair, waiting to pull it out from behind me. I look up and he nods before I take a seat, then he pulls out his chair next to me. I notice filled wine glasses and bread at each setting and if I could will the wine to be directly inserted into my vein, I would.

"Thank you for joining us," Dominic says, turning his head to the left and then again to the right before looking back at me. "Your Majesty." His eyes go to a man directly across from us. "Allow me to introduce Seraph Warrior Gideon."

CHAPTER THIRTY-SIX

GIDEON GIVES ME a slow nod. His handsome, rugged features are sharp and chiseled and his hair is a thick, medium brown. He narrows his hazel-green eyes as if sizing me up…or maybe he just figured out how nervous I actually am. Every single person here is male, each is at least one double my size and they all look like they're hungry for war.

"Your Majesty, it is a pleasure to meet you." Gideon's gritty voice floods the room. He props his elbows on the table and leans forward like he's eager to hear what Dominic has to say.

Dominic shifts in his seat and I look over at him, giving him my full attention. "I have gathered you all here because we have a potential situation that will become volatile of we do not act quickly." He pauses and glances at me before continuing. "The Queen's close friend, Skylar Bennett, is being targeted by several Earth Demons. The details as to why are not important; he needs our immediate protection before they succeed in taking him."

Low murmuring breaks out amongst the other men. My eyes flash across to Gideon and then to a few other men who look completely thrilled at the possibility of confronting Demons. But I can't feel happy for them. I've seen and even spoken to two different ones up close and it wasn't enjoyable and I have a bad feeling in my gut.

"Yes," Dominic interrupts and the room goes quiet as they all look up. "I will need each and every one of you, at some point and time, to help." He looks around, specifically to the men in brown cloaks. "Fighters, Gideon has been assigned as Lead Warrior. He and I will rely on your ability to close in on the Guard Demons surrounding Skylar Bennett's house. You have my permission to do what is necessary, including stopping any attempt of a kidnapping." He takes a drink of the red wine from the glass in front of him. "In addition, you will brief him on any crucial information before the Warriors attack and vanquish the Earth Demons for good."

Holy…

I begin mentally counting the men in black cloaks versus the men in brown. There are six in black, which also means there are only six Warriors. The familiar prickly needles are back, poking away at my gut. All the rest of the men are in brown.

Gideon stands, unrolling a large map across the table and I see the word "Bennett" written in the center over what looks like the roof of a house. The men gather around him as he points out back alleys and side streets for better surveillance.

Dominic must have picked up on my anxiety because he turns to me and whispers, "Do not worry. This is what I have trained for all my life. It is what we have all trained for." His eyes have a certain glow about them—like he can't wait to fight—and I close my eyes.

The last thing I want is for him to go into some kind of battle…hell, I don't want any of them to fight if they don't have to. "Can the Fighters do what you can do?" I whisper, hoping for good news.

"No, but they can even the battleground for us no matter how many Earth Demons show up."

Gulp.

"Are you saying they can't kill?"

"Yes, they can," he stops and takes my hand, "but only the Guard Demons. That is why it is imperative to have as many Warriors prepared as possible."

My eyes go wide. "There are only six at this table!" I hiss, trying not to draw attention as the men continue to strategize.

"If need be, we can summon more, but we will have to get permission from the Council," he says, taking another drink of wine as the servers enter the room with trays of food.

Hmm. "Under what circumstance would there be a need for more Warriors?" I ask, barely getting the words out over the growing nausea.

Dominic's lips tighten and I can tell he doesn't want to answer. He looks around the table before whispering, "If they kill too many..." He pauses for a second. "Or all the Warriors."

Dominic clears his throat, pulling his eyes from mine as he looks back to Gideon. "I recommend you assign shifts to watch over the Bennett family home. Five Seraph Fighters at a time." He looks around the table again. "Obviously, you will need to be cloaked at all times so no one will see you. Once we know the Demons' habits and have a better timeframe of when they plan to take Skylar, a Fighter should be sent back to inform the rest of the Warriors."

Gideon nods in acknowledgement and straightens up in his chair. "If everything goes to plan, there will be no need for a battle." He glances around the table at his men, like he's warning them to use good judgment. "That will be our first priority. Dominic will stay with the Queen unless we require him."

I perk up, reminding myself not to smile because this is a serious dinner. But why the hell didn't Dominic tell me that in the first place?

Dominic's eyes flash; he wasn't expecting that last part. "The Queen can be protected by another Warrior," he says in a low voice. "It is my duty to be prepared at all times."

Gideon leans closer to Dominic, his voice low, like he's trying to keep the conversation from getting out of control. "The Council is forbidding your involvement," he says softly. "Unless we have no other choice."

Dominic rubs his jaw, frustrated. He wants to join them, he wants to fight, that much is clear. He takes another drink as Gideon leans back in his chair.

"After dinner, we will meet in the Great Hall for shift assignments," Gideon announces. "We will begin protecting the Bennett home straight away."

Once the last course has been placed on the table, I can practically slice the tension between Dominic and Gideon. I'm beginning to wonder if something else is going on between them.

The low murmuring in the room goes quiet when Gideon places his napkin on the table and scoots back in his chair. "Your Majesty," he bows his head, "it was a pleasure."

Dominic quickly responds, tossing his napkin down and glancing over to me for the first time since he and Gideon had words. It's as though he forgot I was sitting next to him and my heart drops. Is he seriously that focused on fighting that he can remove me from his mind so easily? I can feel the heat rushing to my cheeks and his eyes instantly go to mine. His face tightens, like he's just realizing the error of his ways and he offers me his arm. I take it because it's what I'm supposed to do but it doesn't matter now because I'm no longer hurt, I'm freaking pissed out of my mind.

"I need to have a word with Gideon. I will not be long," he says as soon as we leave the dining room. He drops my arm before I can even say anything and I watch him stop Gideon.

"I will speak to the Council and—" Dominic gets out but he's interrupted.

"It has already been decided," Gideon says in a warning voice. "I will only tell you this once because I am not sure my tongue could acknowledge it again." He takes in a deep breath like he's trying to stay calm. "You have proven to me and to everyone here that you are our best and most fierce fighter. You are too valuable to the Realm. We have other capable men willing and qualified to do the job."

Dominic stares at him for a few seconds as if contemplating his next move or maybe what his next words will be. "I only did it to teach you," he bites out, clearly talking about something entirely different.

Gideon's eyes dart to the men walking by and then back to Dominic. "And as much as I hate to admit it, you made me a better Warrior because of it. Now allow us to do our duty. Your Queen needs your protection."

Dominic whips his head to me, tightening his lips, before looking back to Gideon. "You are right." He closes his eyes and bows his head, finally realizing what a complete jerk he's being. "Brief me before the Fighters leave."

Gideon gives him a quick nod and Dominic turns back to me. I can already see the apology in his eyes but I'm so mad I can't even look at him.

He takes my arm gently. "Forgive me," he whispers, and the sincerity in his voice practically punches me in the gut. "I...I do not have an excuse for my actions." He moves his head, trying to get me to look at him. "Kate, please." His voice is soft and pleading, like his life depends on it, so I finally allow my eyes to go to his. "I am a Warrior and the need to fight with my men is strong. You know this. It is all I have ever known, all I have ever wanted to do." He reaches for my hand. "But now," he blinks and I swear I see wetness on his cheek, "it is clearer to me now than ever. I must put aside my ego and place you and your needs even before my own." His fingers reach up, tenderly pushing back the strands of hair covering the side of my face. "I will never deny you again. You have my word."

Well, shit...

The anger that consumed me only seconds ago washes away like it was never there. I'm not sure if he did it or I just forgave him on my own but he meant every single word he said. There's no way I can stay mad, this moment is suddenly too special. I have to break down my walls too and kill the ridiculous pride that has led me to so many stupid decisions and unnecessary heartache.

It's time. It's just time.

Reaching up, I touch his face and watch his eyes close as he turns in to kiss my palm—and that's when I feel it. A shift, or maybe a transformation somehow in our relationship. It feels stronger, deeper, even more compassionate. Almost like I've finally broken a wild horse that no one else could—and he's finally mine, *all* mine.

"Guess I'm not the only one who has some learning to do." I give him a slight grin and the relief in his eyes completely changes his expression, making my forgiveness even sweeter. All I want to do is make this man happy. I don't care if I'm giving in too easily and I don't care if we still have so much more to learn because if I can get him to look at me just once more the way he's looking at me right now, every single thing I've gone through in my life will be worth it.

He pulls me close and I slip my arms under his warm cloak, breathing in his amazing rosemary and musk scent. We stay like this for a few more blissful seconds before he whispers, "Come on, my love, I will escort you back to our quarters."

CHAPTER THIRTY-SEVEN

Z ACK SITS IN a wingback next to the fireplace, engaged in a concerned conversation with someone I can't see.

Holy hell, what now?

"Kate!" Aunt Kelly leaps out of the chair and throws her arms around my neck. "I...I'm so sorry! So very sorry, honey." Her breath catches and she whispers, "I...I didn't know."

I pull back because I have no idea what she's talking about, and before I can ask she says, "Zack told me." She looks to the ground and then back up at me. Her eyes are wet and bloodshot. "He—he told me about John a-and, and," she stutters before finishing her thought, "what he did to you."

Oh shit, is she talking about what I think she's talking about?

The guilty look on Zack's face says it all. He told her about Uncle John's perverted, late night attempts to have sex with me. I'm not sure if I'm more upset that he betrayed my trust or if I'm simply mortified that the man I love is about to know. I'm not ready for him to find out. Not yet, and maybe not ever. He'll think I'm disgusting or worse, just as big a monster as Uncle John himself. I have to convince Zack to take it back. I have to make him say he misunderstood me. *Yes, that's it,* he heard me wrong. People make mistakes all the time. Besides, it's not like Uncle John ever got very far, and sometimes he was really nice to me. When he wasn't staggering drunk.

But still.

"I don't know what you're talking about," I blurt out, giving Zack my best "how could you" look. He walks toward me and I shift my eyes back to Aunt Kelly, "He's lying; he's always hated Uncle John."

"Kate," Zack says so low it barely reaches my ears.

"No, it's a lie," I bite out, trying like hell not to look at Dominic. "He's never gotten along with Uncle John, you know that! And now he's just being vindictive!"

Aunt Kelly's eyes spill over as she pulls me into a tight hug, the same tight hug she's always so good at giving. That's when it happens. That's when I fall apart and begin sobbing like a five-year-old kid.

It's out in the open.

They all know.

"Oh, sweet girl, why didn't you come to me?" she whispers in a shaky voice that only I can hear. "Honey, I could have protected you."

My eyes are still closed. I pretend Aunt Kelly's arms are my mother's and more tears stream down my cheeks. I can hear my brother and Dominic murmuring only steps away and I finally look up to see a blurry Dominic staring at me as Zack fills him in. The look in his eyes is pure rage. Now his image of me is forever changed. He must think I'm damaged goods and honestly, I wouldn't blame him for wanting a do over in the love department.

Swallowing a hiccup, I pull away from Aunt Kelly. The second I do, Dominic rushes over and takes me in his arms. "It is not your fault, Kate," he whispers, his palms cupping my face. "You must remember that. Your uncle was a monster before he was possessed by one." His words cut at my heart but the relief is somehow sweet because I know he's right. The fact that Uncle John was so easily influenced by the Demon makes perfect sense. "You must convince your Aunt to allow us to interrogate him again," he says in a low voice. "If the Demon is indeed still inside him, he could still be of use to us."

"Oh, I give you my full permission," Aunt Kelly cuts in. "And I want to be there when you do. That son of a bitch is already dead to me." The pure hatred in her voice like nothing I've ever heard from her before.

"No!" Zack whips his head at Aunt Kelly. "You can't be there, it's too risky."

"Why?" she asks, her confused expression revealing her tempered frustration. "I'm not kidding, Zack, I want the asshole to rot in hell!" Flames practically shoot out of her mouth. "It was bad enough he drained our bank account and treated me like total shit. But it's an entirely different thing to molest an innocent girl," she wipes the spit from her mouth, "who also happens to be my…my fucking niece for Christ's sake!"

"You can't handle it, that's why! You'd be way too emotional!" Zack bites out, looking around the room as if suddenly realizing he's shouting as loudly as she was. "We can't have you changing your mind. You're too close to him." He begins to pace. "I'm sorry, but you haven't seen him the way we have. If Uncle John really is still possessed, the Demon will quickly pick up on your indecisiveness and your emotional weakness." He stops where he is and looks her dead on. "That's how it works with them. That's how they gain their power. They'll play dirty and use everything they can to manipulate you and everyone else in the room."

"B-but," Aunt Kelly hesitates for a second like she's just been punched in the face by reality, "I-I'm sure now." Her voice only a whisper and it's clear even to me she's not as strong as she needs to be. At least not when it comes to Uncle John. Hell, forty-eight hours ago she begged me to bring him back.

"He's right, Aunt Kelly," I whisper, watching her face fall at my words. "This is something I need to do," I walk closer and take her hand, "for me."

She looks away and blinks madly, like she's trying with everything she has to hold back new tears. "Then promise me something," she says, her voice cracking. "Make sure that bastard suffers for what he did to you."

I give her a slight smile, the kind of understanding smile you give someone whose heart is breaking. And not for the man she's been married to for fifteen years—it's breaking because of her love for me. "I'm pretty sure he already has," I whisper, squeezing her hand.

Aunt Kelly squeezes my fingers back before letting go and robotically takes a seat in front of the fireplace again. The dazed look on her face showcases just how defeated she must feel and I'm sad for her all over again.

"Then it's settled," Zack interrupts, focused on the mission. "We'll interrogate the Dem—" He stops himself. "I mean, Uncle John, and hopefully get some answers once and for all."

Dominic has been silent for a while, so when I feel his hand slipping around my waist I'm comforted by the warmth of his body so close to mine. "In the morning," he says in a low voice, looking directly at Zack. "The Queen needs to rest—we all do."

"Yes. Yes, of course," Zack says, stopping his pacing long enough to look up at Dominic. "Before I go, I understand there was some tension between you and Gideon at the Warrior meeting."

Dominic looks from me to Zack before answering. "It has been settled," he replies, his clipped words sending a message that he doesn't want to discuss it.

"Good, we need to keep our wits about us at all times. There's no room for personal ego." I can tell Dominic didn't like that last part—not even a little bit—but he wisely stays quiet. "When will Gideon send the Fighters to start their surveillance on the Bennett House?"

Dominic walks over to the door and pulls up the latch for Zack to go. "Soon. He will inform me the moment they leave."

Zack nods, letting out a slow, deep breath. He must have taken the hint because he looks over to Aunt Kelly, still sitting in the chair staring at the wall like she's in deep thought.

"C'mon, I'll escort you back to your quarters." He reaches for her hand, pulling her out of her daze and guiding her towards the door. "See you in the morning," he says to me, then nods to Dominic, who nods back, still holding on to the latch.

"Goodnight, brother."

Zack offers his hand in apology and Dominic takes it, shaking twice before letting go. Aunt Kelly looks back at me over her shoulder. I wave, watching her smile, but the worry is already there. It's pretty clear we both know how hard tomorrow will be.

I watch as she and Zack fade down the hallway. Dominic gently closes the door and looks over to me. The expression on his face is drenched with confusion, or maybe concern, like he's troubled about something else.

"What is it?"

Oh, no.

"You can't stand the sight of me now." I whisper, walking away from him.

"No!" he yanks my arm but I can tell he didn't mean to do it so forcefully. "What your uncle did to you wasn't your fault. You have to know that."

"All I know is he made me feel dirty. How can you not think the same thing?"

"Kate," he cups my face, "Look at me," my eyes slowly meet his, "You have and always will be my first and true love. Nothing, not your uncle or even a Demon can ever change the way I feel about you. Ever.

He steps closer, taking my fingers in his and draws me close. "Please," he kisses my lips, "Do not ever doubt me."

He means every word he just said and I hug him hard. I needed to hear those words. I needed to have his reassurance. I look up into his eyes and he smiles, but there's still something troubling him. I can feel it and without thinking, I pull away. "What is it? What else is wrong?"

"It is nothing."

"Dominic."

"All right." He keeps his eyes on me, "I am used to planning strategies with my men, I cannot lie." He pauses and his brow furrows as he tries to find the right words. "Although I—" his face lightens up, "I want to be by your side...*more*." He accentuates the last word in a hushed voice, like he's just had an epiphany.

Relieved, I slip my hands around his waist again. "Are you saying I've finally tamed your constant need for battle?"

He grins slightly. "Maybe. I am not completely sure." He leans down and kisses my neck. "I think you know I will always be a Warrior. It is in my blood." He kisses the other side of my neck. "But maybe the only battle I will fight from now on will just be for you."

I chuckle under my breath. "I'm not sure you can handle it. I'm pretty tough."

"Yes," he tenderly kisses my lips, "I noticed."

CHAPTER THIRTY-EIGHT

THREE QUICK KNOCKS at the door startle me out of Dominic's amazing, deep, kiss and all I want to do is throw something at the person who did it.

"Your Majesty?" Victoria peeks her head in the room. "Can I get you anything before you retire?" She addresses me, but her eyes are on Dominic.

"No!" I speak so quickly, but it's obvious what we were doing before she barged in. And she knows it. "Thank you, Victoria." I don't want to fight with her or start any more trouble, but I do want her to understand that unless I need her, stay out. Of course, this isn't the appropriate time for that conversation so I smile and say, "I'll see you in the morning."

Victoria grins and nods to Dominic before dropping into a full bow, escaping out the door.

And again, everything just got super awkward.

"It is getting late," Dominic whispers.

"No," I whine, my arms tightening around his waist. "Stay a little longer."

He shakes his head, gently pulling my arms away, and steps back.

Now it's official, I want to kill Victoria. Mood killer.

"We have a difficult day ahead of us—you should go to bed." His voice is still low and hushed as he turns around.

I take his hand, stopping him, and he looks down at me. "I'm not sure how long I can keep stopping..." I look away, blushing, "without it physically hurting."

He blinks, caught off guard. "It is excruciating," he says under his breath, letting go of my hand and leaving anyway.

I'm not sure if I want cry or feel elated that he's just as torn. Either way, tonight's the first night I wish like hell we were already married.

I must have been more tired than I thought because I don't even remember falling asleep. Light streams through the floor-to-ceiling windows and I yank myself up into a sitting position.

Holy crap, it's already tomorrow?

"Good morning, Your Highness," comes Victoria's cheery voice. "I trust you slept well?"

I look around blearily for a moment before I find her standing at the armoire, laying out clothes on the bench at the foot of the bed. "Yeah. Yeah, I think I did, thanks," I say, rubbing my eyes.

"I'm happy to hear it." She smiles and I can't help wondering if she's actually being sincere. She seems friendly, but I don't know her well enough to know for sure. I watch her for a second, studying her body language and facial expressions.

"I've already drawn you a bath," she comments without looking up. She's going back and forth between the armoire and bench, comparing jewelry with the gown she laid out.

"Thank you." I push back my covers, looking up when she stops and turns around, startled.

"Oh—it is my pleasure, your Majesty." She looks away. Between that and her surprised "oh," I figure she's not used to anyone thanking her.

Well, hell, now I feel a little sorry for her.

"So, tell me," I say, because now I'm curious, "before I came into the Realm, were you someone else's Follower?"

"Yes," she says, continuing to compare earrings with the necklace she picked out. "I am still in his service."

"His?"

She nods and my stomach flies up to my throat. Please *do not* tell me it's for him. I can't take another surprise. Not today, not before I have to face Uncle John.

"Yes." Her brows push together like she thought I already knew. "I am also Zack's Follower."

Wait, what?

I don't try to hide my relief, though I do have to stop myself from running up and hugging the crap out of her. "My brother? You're his Follower, too?"

"Yes. It is not a secret," she adds. "I have been his Follower since he arrived several months ago." She stops and I can tell she's holding something back. "However, he no longer requires much of my time." She looks away, making me think there's more to this story.

"I'm sure he's pretty busy. Especially now that I'm here," I say, watching her eyes come back to me.

"Yes. H-he's very busy," she says, but the hurt behind her eyes is crystal clear.

Holy shit, she's in love with him...

It makes sense, if I stop and think about it. Her eyes always stay on him just a little longer than necessary. And it could also explain some of the tension I've noticed between Dominic and Zack. But why didn't Dominic tell me? We could have avoided so much of our own drama had I known how she felt about my brother.

Can Zack really be that clueless? Maybe Zack doesn't even know? Is it a secret? It is a forbidden relationship?

I should probably slow down my thoughts. If I want to get more information, I need to be subtle about this. I know there's more to this story and I'm pretty sure I'll be able to get her to talk. Hell, just knowing she's no longer after Dominic makes me want to help her.

"Thank you for the bath," I say slipping into the tub instead of asking one of the questions jumping around in my head. The lavender-scented bubbles are as relaxing as the soothing water. I rest my head against the bath pillow, completely covered in white, fluffy clouds. I can't help wondering if this is the calm before the storm. I have to face my uncle, the man who drained Aunt Kelly of all her savings, selfishly gambling every penny away. The same man who also attempted, on several occasions, to touch me. I'll never forget the sheer disgust on her face or the immense pain in her eyes. Dominic was right; Uncle John is a monster and Demon or not, he doesn't deserve to live.

The door flies open and I jerk, sitting up as thick suds pop all around me.

"Majesty!" Victoria screams. "It's—it's—come quickly!" She starts to cry.

Grabbing the robe from the side of the tub, I throw it on, almost slipping on the stone floor. "What's wrong?" I try not to yell as I tie the belt around my waist, following Victoria as she rushes out of the bathroom.

Zack calmly meets me at the door. "Katie, something has happened." I watch a tear roll down his cheek. "It's about…

225

dammit," he curses under his breath, shaking his head. "It's Aunt Kelly." His eyes meet mine. "She's…she's gone."

"What do you mean, she's gone?" I ask, denying what I can already see in his eyes. I can't accept anything worse.

I won't.

"H-how did she find her way out?" My words come out in a whisper as I try like hell to fabricate a different scenario.

I can't face it. It can't be true.

"Sit down." Zack guides me to the wingback by the freshly-lit fire and kneels in front of me, taking both of my hands. "S-she…took her life last night."

I don't think I heard him correctly. She didn't take her life. I won't allow his words into my head; they aren't true. This can't be happening. I just talked to her; her arms were around me only hours ago. She was fine. She was prepared to fight. She was fine.

Or at least I thoughts she was.

Movement to my right makes me look up to see Dominic fly through the bedroom door, rushing to my side. He yanks me up in his arms, his cloak wrapping another layer around my body, holding me tighter than he's ever held me before. "Oh, Kate…I am so very sorry," he whispers and I totally fall apart. His hand cups the back of my head as tears cascade down my cheeks.

I don't want to believe it. This has to be a mistake, it has to be.

CHAPTER THIRTY-NINE

"I NEED TO GO to her," I say, pushing away from Dominic as a new thought slams in my head. "I—I can help her!" My voice rises as I try to wiggle my way free from his tight hold.

"Kate." Dominic locks eyes with me, the serious look on his face turning my stomach. "It is too late." His voice is so quiet I have to read his lips. "She has been gone too long."

"No!" I shout, finally getting free. "I need to see her! Now!"

Dominic and Zack exchange a look. "Let her go," Dominic finally says.

They both follow me out the door, Dominic wrapping one side of his massive cloak around my shaky body as he kisses the top of my head. We rush through the long hallways and around two corners before finally reaching the infirmary. I shield my eyes from the bright lights, sagging when I spot the white shrouded body flanked by two brown-cloaked Seraph Fighters on each side, keeping watch.

"Is that," I swallow, "her?" I know it is, but I still look up at Dominic and he nods, tightening his lips.

He glances over to the two men. "Fighters, give us a few minutes."

They both nod and bow before heading for the door, gently closing it behind them.

Zack reaches out and touches my hand. "You don't have to do this," he says, making me pause before stepping toward the body.

I turn and look up at him. "Yes. Yes, I do." My voice cracks. "I have to say goodbye." I can already feel my legs starting to give out as I begin to lift a corner of the thin white sheet.

"Wait," Zack orders and I drop my hand. "I—I'll do it." He steps forward, wiping his eyes as he slowly pulls back the sheet.

The first thing I see is Aunt Kelly's face—still beautiful but different somehow. Like she's finally at peace and the worry that was always hidden so deeply inside her has been completely erased. I'm almost relieved for her. My knees buckle slightly when I touch her soft cheek. I know there's nothing to be done. Even I can't save her. I lean back, letting Dominic's warm hands support me, keeping me steady as I try to catch my breath.

"How did she—" I stop to blink away the well of new tears, but when I try to speak again nothing comes out.

Zack swallows hard and without a word, pulls the sheet back a little further and I gasp at the deep, angry gashes on her wrists.

Something is terribly wrong. It isn't just her death, it's how. My blood heats; I feel like I'm on some kind of autopilot, growing and becoming stronger. Maybe I'm in shock, maybe this is how the new me reacts, but falling apart isn't the answer. Not now. Not when I can rip the person who killed her to shreds.

"She didn't do this—it wasn't her," I blurt out.

"We know," Dominic says in a low voice.

"Then why aren't we looking for the person who did?!" I shout, yanking away from Dominic's warm embrace. I'm so furious and want to take a bat to every single thing in this room.

"You know exactly who made her do it, Katie," my brother whispers, the tone of his voice making it so clear that instant fury, like hot lava, begins to pour through my veins.

Uncle John. The Demon is still inside him.

"There are only a few ways to kill an immortal and draining their blood is one of them." Zack whispers. "You and I both know she wouldn't have done this on her own. Somehow he got in her head. Somehow he influenced her."

I can feel my nostrils flaring and the lava rushing to my face. ""Take me to him now," I order, my voice so calm even I'm stunned by it.

"No! Not now." Zack raises his voice. "You're too..." He reaches out and takes me by the shoulders, resting his forehead against mine. "Katie, it's too dangerous in your state right now. Look what he's already done!" He tries to convince me, but none of his words are reaching my sensibilities.

I pull away, knowing I have the upper hand. I can decide right here, right now what I want and neither he nor Dominic can stop me. "Take me to that fucking monster so I can make him suffer so much, he'll beg me to kill him."

"Katie, wait—think about this for a minute," Zack implores. "This is exactly what the Demon wants. He wants you to attack him. He wants you to be emotionally unbalanced—that's how they win. That's how he got to Aunt Kelly. You have to be smart about this."

It's all I can do to even hear half the words coming out of my brother's mouth, but somehow, somewhere deep inside me, I know he's right. I'm so enraged I literally see everything in bright red, and if I go to Uncle John now, I would only be putting myself and everyone around me in danger. I have to get ahold of my emotions first. I have to stop making bad decisions because of them. Even though right now all I want to do is rip that asshole from limb to limb, I need to step back, I need to get ahold of myself.

The look of concern on both of their faces only confirm that I'm right and I walk away, trying to calm the fury still bubbling inside of me. I know what I need to do. I would never forgive myself if I didn't take the time to do it now. I turn around and look them both in the eye as the raging heat inside me subsides, "C-can I have as second with her? Alone?"

Without a word, Dominic and Zack look at each other and then quietly walk out of the room. The silence after the door gently closes is deafening, making having to say goodbye to Aunt Kelly even more heart wrenching.

I take a few steps closer, gently touching her light brown hair. A single tear escapes down my cheek as I whisper, "I'm sorry. I'm so sorry I wasn't there for you. Had I known…" I stop to wipe away another tear. "I…I could have done something differently, I could have stopped you." I take in a quick breath, trying so hard not to break down. "And even though I didn't live with you long, I knew you loved me. I will never forget that. I promise you, I will get the son-of-a-bitch who did this to you." I hiccup, choking back more tears. "I…I hope you know how much I loved you. I always will, Aunt Kelly."

Saying her name makes it more real and suddenly, I have to throw up. I almost trip over my own feet on the way to the nearest trash can, then have to force myself to stop heaving after a minute or two. Shaking, I wipe my mouth on the sleeve of my bathrobe before returning to Aunt Kelly's body. I slowly lean down, gently kissing her cheek as the tip of my fingers take the edges of the sheet and pull it back over her pretty face. I know this will be the last time I'll ever see her…the last time I can actually touch her… Without thinking, I cry out and yank back the stupid white sheet, pulling her into my arms. I rock her back and forth as warm rivers of tears flow down my neck.

"I'll never forget you. Forgive me." I squeeze as tightly as I can because those were the kinds of hugs she liked—and now, they're the only kind I'll ever give.

CHAPTER FORTY

I'M NOT SURE how long I've been holding her, but when I hear footsteps approaching, I don't have to open my eyes to know who it is. The scent of earth and rosemary surround me before I feel his warm hand on my shoulder, stopping my constant rocking.

The gentleness in his movement says enough. I know he can feel what I'm feeling and he slowly moves closer, tenderly taking my arms away and replacing them with his. Slowly, he lays Aunt Kelly's body back down, silently pulling the white sheet back over her. I'm shaking all over and without a word, he scoops me in his arms, cradling me like a baby.

"It is time to go, my love," he says, his voice vibrating on my cheek. "I have you now."

His strong grip and steady pace comfort me as he carries me out of the infirmary. Without warning, images of Aunt Kelly's wrists and how small she looked lying on that gurney slam into my head. I nestle my face harder to his chest, trying like hell to erase her deep gash wounds from my mind. I take in a slow breath, allowing Dominic's earthy scent and the steady rhythm of his movement to soothe my mind, pulling away the dark images of her suicide.

Before I know it, I'm settled in one of the wingbacks next to the fireplace in our room. I sit up and rub my eyes, watching as he pulls the other chair only inches away, taking a seat in front of me.

He reaches for my hand and squeezes tightly. "Are you okay?" he whispers and I nod blankly. "You understand there was nothing you could have done, right?" I can see the sorrow in his eyes. "Your uncle's hold over her was too powerful."

I look away, slamming my lids shut as if it will block out the pain. I know Aunt Kelly would be alive today had I only listened to Dominic. He warned me, even tried to stop me, but I wouldn't have it. I was too stubborn and self-serving, and now I've lost yet another family member. Someone who didn't deserve to die. Someone who had a bigger heart than me.

"You could not have known," he says, his voice so low I have to open my eyes and watch his lips. "It happened the way it was meant to."

I don't reply, waiting for him to go on.

His lips tighten. "She never would have let him go, you know that." He kisses my hand. "And you would have carried the burden of regret for the rest of your life."

"She was ready to," I interrupt, pulling our conversation out of a whisper. "I saw it in her eyes—so did you!"

"She was angry, Kate," he says simply, the wisdom in his tone jarring me out of my self-loathing.

He moves his chair away and gets on his knees, taking both of my hands again in his. "There is a reason she stood by him, even when he foolishly gambled away their money for years. His lack of respect had weakened their marriage and it weakened her in the process. It is clear to me now that had you not brought him back she would have blamed you for his death." He pauses and smiles sympathetically. "Your motive was out of pure intent and because of it, the right outcome prevailed." He leans in and lightly kisses my cheek, looking over my shoulder. "Right will always win, my love."

I follow his eyes as my brother walks in with Victoria following. Zack jerks his head to the right.

Dominic instantly releases my hands. "Be right back," he whispers as Victoria bends into a full bow in front of me.

"Your Majesty, I am so very sorry for your loss," she says. "How can I help you?"

The sadness in her eyes is genuine but something tells me she's trying to divert my attention from Dominic and Zack. Or maybe something else has happened. I'm getting a bad feeling and as soon as Victoria straightens up I glare at her.

"What's going on now?" I ask, watching her eyes go to Zack and then back to me.

"Nothing to concern yourself with, your Majesty. Are you hungry?" She clears her throat. "Thirsty?" Victoria's terrible attempt at masking the truth sends needles to my gut and I practically jump out of my chair to get to Dominic.

"Somebody better start talking—" I get out before Zack interrupts me.

"It's Uncle John," he says in a warning voice and the needles poke a little harder. "We've had him sedated since we found Aunt Kelly, but he won't last long in this state."

Without thinking, I blurt out, "Good, let the asshole die."

Zack shakes his head. "I wish it were that easy," he admits. "We need information out of him, Katie. We cannot forget that Skylar is in danger. If the Demon can tell us anything about what they're planning to do with him, we need to know."

Holy shit, I almost forgot about Skylar.

At least now I can focus on something else besides my sadness. I'm on a mission. I won't allow the death of another person, especially not one I love. Not on my watch and hopefully not ever again. "What are we waiting for? Let's go."

Dominic pulls me back by the arm. "Kate," he whispers, "I am not sure you are ready."

I can already feel the blood rushing to my face, "Oh, you have no idea how ready I am. I refuse to keep running away when things get too intense. I have to do this don't you see? And I'd rather do it with you than without you." My eyes go back and forth between Dominic and Zack, who are now grinning back at me. I'm not sure if I've convinced them or...I look down. I'm still in my bathrobe.

Crap.

"Hold up," Zack says, stopping me from rushing toward Victoria already standing at the armoire. "We must prepare ourselves first."

He knows I have the last word on this and I'm relieved he's not going to fight me, but maybe he's right. One thing I've learned on this crazy journey is that it's probably a good idea to listen before my anger overrides my decision making.

"Okay." I look up at Dominic, who still doesn't look convinced, before glancing back at my brother. "What do we need to do?"

He smiles like he's relieved I'm actually listening this time and looks over to Dominic. "Let Victoria help her get changed, then take her to the Chapel. I will gather the supplies we need and meet you there shortly."

Dominic nods as Zack leaves the room and then looks back to me. "You do not have to do this, Kate. There is no question the Demon is still in control of your uncle."

"Oh, I'm fully aware the Demon's still there," I say smartly, thinking of all the ways I want to kill the man and the monster. "But that's not going stop me from playing with my new toy."

CHAPTER FORTY-ONE

I CAN TELL HE doesn't approve of my choice of words.

"This is not a game, Kate," he says, his cautious tone reminding me of his love.

I reach up, cupping his face to bring his eyes back to me. "I know that, but if I can get some kind of retaliation, some kind of revenge…" I stop when I hear my own words out loud. That isn't right. I have to stop thinking of just myself. I'm starting to realize that now.

He knows. He knows I'm trying to slow my wheels from spinning. I have to start listening; I have to start asking the right questions.

"How can I keep from losing my temper?" I ask. "I'm still so angry with him, or the Demon, hell, whatever he is."

He smiles a little, his eyes glowing with sympathy, and places his hand over mine. "You must throw away all of your preconceived notions about your uncle. He *is* the Demon now. There is no saving the man that he used to be."

"I don't want to save him, not at all." I pause as the memory of what he did tears through me. "What I would like to do is cut off his—"

"That is just it, Kate," Dominic interrupts. "If you allow him to get to you, you are handing over every ounce of your power."

He's right. I know he's right. I have to focus on Skylar and how I can help him. Even though Uncle John abused me, even though he treated his wife like shit, now a Demon has taken over his body. I need to keep Skylar a priority. I can't change what Uncle John did as himself or under the influence of the Demon, but I can at least stop the Demon from doing any more harm.

The doors to the armoire close, diverting our attention. Victoria appears in from behind it, all business. "Your Highness, I have your dress ready. We must get you dressed."

I look down, forgetting once again that I'm still wearing a bathrobe and glance back at Dominic. "I'll hurry."

"I will be by your side the whole time," he whispers, tenderly kissing the top of my head. "Now go. Zack is waiting."

"Be right back," I say over my shoulder as I bolt toward Victoria. "And Dominic," I stop and look back to him, "thank you."

"For what?"

I take a second and really look at him. The handsome features of his chiseled face and the wisdom of so many years behind his eyes, as he stands, ready to fight for me no matter how unsure I am of myself. "For believing in me."

He grins, his face lighting up as he bows his head but this time, not because I'm his Queen, but because he loves me.

Victoria clears her throat, already holding up my gown as I follow her to the bathroom. "Here you are, Majesty," she says with a troubled smile.

I think she's worried for me and I can't help but like her more for it. Dropping the white robe, I raise my arms so she can slip the beautiful sapphire fabric over my head.

"I may be a little overdressed," I whisper as she zips up the back.

"You are the Queen," she reminds me. "There are no other garments."

"Maybe you should order me a pair of jeans and a t-shirt." I stop in mid-thought because this formal crap is getting weird. "And please, just call me Kate."

"Oh, no, I cannot do that." She guides me to the chair and brushes out my long auburn hair. "It is against the rules."

"Even if I say it's okay?"

Victoria nods. "It is important for everyone to understand their place in the Realm," she answers, reaching for the matching sapphire earrings. "Respect above everything else is what is most important. A child would not call his or her parents by their first names, right?" She looks to me inquiringly and I shake my head. "Same basic principle."

"Kate," Dominic's voice suddenly comes from the other side of the bathroom door, "we must go."

I jump up and Victoria steps back, curtseying into a full bow. "You will be in my thoughts, your Majesty."

"I appreciate it."

Dominic takes my hand as I emerge from the bathroom, his expression catching me by surprise. "You look stunning," he whispers, kissing the tips of my fingers.

"I feel like I'm going to a formal ball instead of some kind of standoff with a Demon," I comment as we walk together down the hallway, my arm tucked in his.

"The Queen will always be dressed appropriately to her status," he says in a low voice, keeping his eyes straight ahead, already on guard. "The chapel is just ahead to the right. We must stay as quiet as possible and allow the Seraph Minister to perform the cleansing ceremony."

I stop and pull at his arm. "Cleansing ceremony? Please tell me I'm not going to be dunked into a tub of water."

Dominic grins. "No, nothing like that. This will be the easy part." His voice is only a whisper as we approach the chapel doors.

The gold arches etched on the doors are breathtaking, with engraved angels surrounding each corner, similar to the Seraph Council doors. I'm caught staring when Dominic pushes one side open, allowing me to walk through. White candles of every shape and size are the only light in the room, giving it an immediate feeling of comfort and peace.

A man, wearing a white cloak bows before me. "Hello, Your Majesty." When he stands and looks up, I can't help noticing his gray mustache and beard. It's the first time I've ever seen anyone look over thirty in this place. "I am Pastor Ezekiel," he says, his voice so soothing I could listen to it all day. "Please join your brother."

My eyes follow his outstretched hand to Zack, kneeling in front of a small, bird feeder-like fountain. Without speaking, Dominic and I walk over, lowering to our knees next to him.

The Pastor begins speaking in some other language, the same language I've heard Dominic speak in. "*Patre cum illis ut faciem daemonis…*" he says, sprinkling us with water from a white bottle with a gold cross on the front. "*Bonitatem et prevalebis victum malis.*" He touches each one of our foreheads. "Now drink from the fountain." He cups his hands in the water, bringing it to our mouths one by one. "*Vincere potest nisi rectum…* Amen."

I'm actually surprised when I feel more peaceful…even cleansed somehow. Like all the negativity surrounding me has been somehow washed away. I'm not sure I would have believed it had I not felt it myself but it's a welcome sensation and I'm grateful for what Pastor Ezekiel has given me.

"You are ready now," the Pastor finally says, looking down at us. "And may peace be with you..."

As soon as Zack gets up, Dominic and I do the same, watching the Pastor disappear behind one of the fully lit candelabras. Quietly, Dominic and I follow Zack back into the dimly lit hallway.

"There is something you must know," Zack says, his face becomes serious. "Uncle John no longer looks like himself."

"What do you mean?" I reach for Dominic and he takes my hand.

"He has transformed almost fully into the Demon," he explains, his voice low and hushed. "It happened after Aunt Kelly..." He stops himself before continuing. "It...it might be better this way."

"You mean it'll be easier to kill him if he no longer looks like our relative?"

"Exactly," Zack says, rubbing the side of his face.

"At this point, it really doesn't matter," I reply. "Let's see what the bastard knows."

Zack nods, turning down the dark hallway. Dominic squeezes my hand hard. It's time.

"One more thing." Dominic looks down, as if wishing he didn't have to tell me. "You brought him back." He whispers, "So only you can kill him."

What the...

I don't have time to be pissed but I don't try to hide my sarcasm. "That would have been beneficial information like, yesterday."

Dominic's expression gets more intense. "If I had told you before now, the worry would have consumed you." He whis-

241

pers, trying to keep his voice down but Zack stops, turning around to see what's going on. "You have the full ability to do it, Kate, and we will be by your side when you are ready.

"We need to hurry," Zack says, snapping us out of our argument.

Without a word, I drop Dominic's hand and turn to follow my brother. A few steps later, I feel his fingers slip through mine again. I know it's Dominic's way of apologizing. I can't be mad, not now. My focus has to stay on helping Skylar. So I wrap my fingers around his massive ones without looking up and we make our way down the familiar hallway to the metal room.

The maze of corridors is getting easier to navigate. Now I know when to turn and which way to go without thinking. We're getting close, I can almost feel the demon.

The thick steel door is just how I remember it, gunmetal gray and at least four inches thick. Zack opens the combination latch with practiced ease; he doesn't seem nearly as nervous as I feel.

The eerie silence that follows us in sends chills up my arms, but it's short-lived. We barely get inside before laughter completely floods the room.

"I thought you'd never get here!" the Demon calls out.

He's in a sturdy wooden chair, completely bound and chained to the floor. Zack was right, he looks nothing like Uncle John. His eyes are completely black and his skin has a clammy, yellow hue to it, almost as though the body has already died.

"Zull," my brother wastes no time, "tell us what the Demons want with Skylar Bennett."

Laughter explodes again, echoing off the metal walls, and he smiles, winking at me. "It's a secret."

"Zull, I command you to tell us! Now!" Zack's voice has a more authoritative tone than I've ever heard.

Zull makes a face like he's somehow being physically hurt. "Queen Kate," Zull looks back to me, breathing more heavily, "isn't Skylar *your* friend? The same friend who, by all accounts, stalked you at the cemetery because he's...how do I put this gently in front of your betrothed...still in love with you?"

CHAPTER FORTY-TWO

I KNOW DOMINIC IS looking at me, but I don't dare look up at him. I don't have time to explain that I never felt that way toward Skylar. Besides, aren't we *not* supposed to engage with the Demon? Aren't we supposed to be prepared for the Demon to bait us?

Laughter bursts out of the Demon's mouth again. "Oh, I guess that's news to your little boyfriend."

"It's not news," I spout off, trying to keep ahold of my temper. "It wasn't like that between Skylar and me."

Zull cocks his head. "Are you sure about that?" he asks, his voice dripping in wicked sarcasm.

I pause, reminded of the time Skylar tried to kiss me when I was at his house. *Shit, he's right.* I totally forgot about it until now—and having it revealed in front of the man I love is making it sound so much worse.

"Nothing happened!" I bite out. Zack's hand goes to my shoulder and I know that's my cue to calm down.

"Zull, do not make this harder on yourself," Zack commands, "Tell us what the Demons want with Skylar."

Zull's black eyes flash over to Zack. "It's too late to save him," he says in a voice that sounds like it's strangely echoed and entangled in other voices. "They already have him."

Before I can say anything, Zack jerks his head at Dominic, who rushes out of the room without a single look in my direction. I can't worry about him now. If they really do have Skylar, I'm going to completely lose my shit.

"Aww, Queen Kate, there, there," the Demon says condescendingly. "You would be very proud of him. He's been fully cooperative. A true asset to our cause."

I have to force myself not to tear him apart with my bare hands. I should have left him for dead the first time, no matter what Dominic said about my good intent. "You son of a bitch!" I scream as Zack wraps his arms around me, holding me back.

Zull's eyes stay glued to mine as he stretches his neck, making a sickening popping noise. "And just so you know, I didn't have to coax sweet Kelly much. She was already halfway there when I suggested she cut her other wrist." He laughs, sending bile rushing to the back of my throat.

Zack's hands tighten around my arms. "He's deliberately trying to get to you," he whispers in my ear. "The Demon knows you're the only one who can kill him. Be smart about this, Katie."

I look up into his new blue eyes and nod. He's right. I need to stay focused. I slowly pull my eyes away from Zack and look back to the Demon. "Zull!" I shout, "I command you to tell me where they have taken Skylar!"

Zull growls, as if he suddenly can't stand the sound of my voice, so I try again.

"I command you, Zull, tell me! Tell me!" I shout so loudly my voice cracks, only this time, I didn't say the last part in English—it was full on Latin.

The Demon starts to convulse and Uncle John's already dead-looking flesh begins ripping away from the sockets connecting his arms, spilling out the pungent odor of death. My palm goes to my face as pain overwhelms me.

Zack steps ahead of me, repeating my exact words. *"Tulit autem dic mihi qua* Skylar!"

"Caemeterium..." Zull gets out before thick black liquid shoots straight up from his mouth, forming into the body of giant reptile with horns and spikey hands.

Zack pulls me close as the creature approaches, but I fight my way free, stepping closer to the Demon. I won't get the information I wanted but I won't let him hurt us, either.

"May light prevail over evil as we stand strong and rebuke you, Demon! I banish you back to hell...forever!" I shout, understanding every word I just said again in Latin.

The metal door flies open as Dominic runs in, slamming our bodies down to the floor as the black liquid separates into huge black rocks, swirling violently around us. Dominic crouches down even further, covering us fully with his cloak. One of the rocks pounds his back and another one slams down by his feet. Warm liquid tinged with the scent of copper drips onto my hand. Dominic's blood. I scream his name but he doesn't move, still protecting us from the chaos above.

It feels like an eternity of thunderous beating against the walls as I can only picture scattering boulders flying through the air while smaller chunks continue pounding at Dominic's back. I'm praying so hard to God, or whoever will listen before everything goes quiet and the black shroud of Dominic's cloak is lifted away. The flying rocks have thankfully disappeared and the remains of Uncle John's body are in a pile, dripping grotesquely from the chair. Dominic is crouched a few feet away.

I stumble to my feet, tripping on my dress to get to him. "Dominic! Where are you hurt?" I scream, searching his back for wounds.

"Here!" Zack beats me to it, pointing out the side of Dominic's calf, bleeding profusely all the way down to the exposed broken bone.

"I am okay," Dominic whispers, the pain in his voice thick, "but I need a crystal."

Zack pulls something out of his pant pocket and hands it to Dominic. "You can thank Pastor Ezekiel," he smiles, "It was his idea."

Dominic squeezes the half dollar-sized crystal in his hand, centering it just above his leg. A bright flash of light illuminates the room for less than a second. When I open my eyes, he is completely healed. Even though I knew what would happen I can't deny that it's pretty unbelievable and it's hard not to stare, wondering if my eyes are really just playing tricks on me.

"Zull spoke the truth," Dominic says, pulling my eyes away from his leg. "The Demons have Skylar."

"No!" I shout. "We—we have to find him!"

"The cemetery!" Zack interrupts. "Zull said that's where they've taken him!"

Zack jumps to his feet as Dominic rushes toward the door. "Keep her safe," he says over his shoulder without looking back at me and I scramble to get up, hoping I can stop him.

"Dominic!" I call his name but it's too late. He's gone before I can explain...before I can tell him that Skylar and I are just friends. And now he's gone to fight the Demons. The one thing I tried like hell to stop, the one thing that was once my nightmare, is now a reality.

CHAPTER FORTY-THREE

"HE'LL BE BACK, Katie." Zack reaches over, patting my back as if reading my mind.

"What if he isn't?" I barely get the words out before tears begin streaming down my cheeks. "What if—"

"Katie," he pulls me into a hug, "Dominic is an experienced Warrior and you're forgetting he'll have Gideon and four other Warriors by his side."

"I've s-seen how p-powerful those Demons are," I sputter. "And if they are outnumbered…"

Zack thinks for a moment. "There might be something I can do," he says, grinning like he's pleased with himself. "I can send a Seraph Fighter to help, maybe even two."

"I thought they couldn't kill Demons."

"They can't, but they can stay visible long enough to report back to us. Maybe even distract the Demons long enough to make it a fair fight. I just hope there won't be a need."

Without thinking, I dart for the door.

Zack catches up, blocking my exit. "Where are you going?"

I don't answer, sure he already sees it in my face. "Oh no, Katie, you are not going to the cemetery!"

"Zack, if you don't take me," I glare at him, "then I'll find another way."

"Dammit, Katie!"

I hear him shouting but I'm already running as fast as I can. I don't have time to acknowledge the random people greeting me with hurried bows as I rush by. I've got to get to Dominic. I've got to make him understand. I head straight for the Hall of Warriors, figuring it's the best way to get me directly to the cemetery. Or maybe I missed something the first time; maybe there's another way out?

I've gotten the attention of several Seraph Fighters because a good amount of them are following me. I'm not sure if they're escorting me or tracking me. It doesn't matter because I feel a familiar hand on my shoulder.

"Kate, what are you doing?" Dominic asks.

The relief is overwhelming and I practically leap into his arms. "I—I thought—"

"You have to go back," he whispers in my ear, knowing exactly what I'm up to and my heart pounds a little faster.

"No, I'm going with you!" I cry, kissing his neck as I hug him even tighter.

"There is no way. It is too dangerous." He pulls back, looking me in the eyes. "I will not allow it."

"But, I—I can help!" I plead, hoping he'll listen. "What if…" I pause for a second, changing my strategy. "Skylar won't know anyone, but he'll know me."

He hesitates, taking a deep breath, contemplating his options. He shakes his head. "No, Kate, there are too many of them," he admits as razor sharp needles cut the insides of my gut.

"Too many who?" I ask, swallowing back the dry lump that just formed in my throat.

He looks away, and that's when I know. That's when I know exactly what he meant.

"H-how many Demons are there?" I whisper, bracing for the worst.

He shakes his head again, and I know he doesn't want to share, but when I take his face in my hands his eyes return to me. "Seven," he whispers, closing his eyes.

I have to catch my breath. *Holy mother...*

"Wait, that means...there are only six Warriors," I say under my breath. My mouth goes dry as everything become clear. "It was Uncle John giving the Demons information all along."

Dominic nods and I wrap my arms around his neck again. "Please let me go! I—I know I can help!" I plead again, but I can already feel his arms letting me go.

"No, my love." He releases me and leans down to kiss my forehead. "We have several Fighters on their way." He pauses and I feel his body gearing up for battle. "They will scope the area first, giving us a better advantage. Protecting you is my first priority and this is the safest place."

I hear his words but I don't want to accept them. "But if I can save a life, isn't it worth the risk?" I whisper, reaching for his hand.

"Not when you are our Queen." He brings my hand to his lips, kissing it. "I cannot wait any longer," he says. "I love you." He sprints straight toward the Hall of Warriors.

"Dominic!" I scream, but he doesn't look back. "Wait!" I take off after him and before I know it, I'm grabbing him by the arm as he runs down the black hallway.

"Kate, noooo!"

His hand comes around my waist and another around the back of my head, tucking me in his cloak as we spin our way through a weightless, dark abyss. I try to take a breath but there's no air. It's exactly what happened last time. Panic begins to take over and I struggle to get free but Dominic is way ahead of me, keeping me close as we fly through whatever this dark, lifeless hole actually is. Without warning, we land hard on wet grass but it doesn't matter because I can finally suck in a deep breath of sweet air.

"What have you done?!" Dominic hisses, opening up his cloak and allowing the light from outside to flood all around me.

We've made it to the cemetery. The clouds are thick and there's a slight breeze and I smile to myself. We made it and we're alone...for now.

"They won't know I'm here," I say, looking up at Dominic, who's already on his feet and carrying me behind a clump of trees.

"They can smell you!" he says in a low growl and my stomach drops.

Oh shit.

"I'll hide further away," I assure him and for the first time I can see anger mixed with worry in his eyes.

"That will not help," he bites out as he gathers piles of leaves, twigs and branches, throwing everything on top of me. "Wait. We have to disguise your scent. Take off your grown," he commands.

Wait, what?

"Kate, if you want any chance of surviving, take it off, now!"

The low tone in his voice startles me and without hesitating, I get to my feet and turn around, looking back at him over my shoulder. I catch him staring down at the zipper of my dress and I swear I can actually see the desire in his eyes.

"You'll have to pull it down, I can't do it myself," I admit, embarrassed that the only thing I'm wearing underneath is an almost sheer white slip.

I feel a slight tug at the base of my neck and the sound of the zipper gliding down the small of my back. His warm fingers lightly brush against my flesh as tiny goosebumps cover my body. I turn around to pick it up but he beats me to it, walking away to bury it in the pile of brush.

"Hang on," he says, picking up a handful of slightly damp dirt. "Stand still." He rubs the cool soil on my arms, my neck, my legs. His eyelids grow heavy and his breathing quickens. I can feel it too, and if it weren't for the battle we're about to face, this moment between us would end much differently.

"Kate?" a familiar voice calls my name, "is that you?"

I immediately look to my right and I see Skylar, looking the same as always with tousled hair, standing next to a man I don't recognize. A man who looks normal, but as I look closer, there's something a little off about him. Something I recognize almost instantly.

"This is Zull," Skylar introduces him, "he says he knows you."

End of book 1

Made in the USA
Monee, IL
05 August 2023

40498818R00144